A Story A Day
Keeps the EVIL Away

Michael A. Woll

DEDICATION

*This book is dedicated to
my mother, Pearl Woll
my friend, Tim Barlowe*

A special thanks for all of her contributions to Kathy Kovacic.

Other short story books by Michael A. Woll

Slices of Dark and Light

Tales Told in the Moonlight

website: givemefiveminutes.org

©2014 by Michael A. Woll
ISBN 978-1500874797

INTRODUCTION

Colors of the night dominated my final waking moments. The light blues faded away to the dark purples and deep navys. The starless sky welcomed the blackness enveloping everything and I drifted off to sleep.

Through the clouds of memory and the fog of regret, I dreamed of imaginary people in imaginary worlds: a magician losing his magic, a deal with the devil, a dead body buried in the middle of the night, the mysterious door in the forest, an ex-wife's revenge, a drug addict reflects on his life, and a gangster returns from the dead. Had my world of dreams become unending nightmares? But there stood Detective Sully to save the day. Not all my dreams had surrendered to the dark side of life.

Enter my dreams. Meet these people and others. Experience their successes and struggles. Join me on my journey...

Contents

Mephistopheles	1
Justice For All	7
When The Rains Fell	21
If the Shoe Fits	31
Jesse's Story	41
The Great Waldini	51
Don't Speak Ill of the Dead	63
The Hanging Judge	71
Deadly Desire	83
The Witch's Door	93
Blood Red Roses	101
Boxed In	109
Junior	119
April Fooled	129
A Gift for Santa	137
Rose Among Thorns	145
P R O T O	155
Back from the Dead?	161
The Other Side	171
The Moment	177

Mephistopheles

I sat in the darkness with my newly lit cigar and a glass of forty-year-old Macallan Scotch. Easing back in my comfortable rocking chair I tried to relax. Smooth jazz played through my Bose speakers. Dave Brubeck will be missed in the music world. I wore my navy silk pajamas one last time. My life was ending and I had grown to accept the inevitable event. Will this be my new reality—eternal night?

Dr. Harvey gave me my death sentence. "Sorry, there's nothing left we can do. The cancer has spread throughout your body. Go home. Spend time with your family and friends." I never told anyone. Just a quick smile and reassuring words that everything would be alright. They bought the lie.

Are there days or hours remaining for me? The grandfather clock chimed loudly twelve times, the midnight hour. I drank my expensive Scotch. No reason to save that $10,000 bottle anymore. Nothing to be concerned with since my will and power of attorney were all in place. I waited for my midnight visitor.

I exhaled the cigar smoke into the air. Suddenly two

A Story A Day Keeps the EVIL Away

red eyes appeared out of the blackness of my family room. "Mephistopheles, I wondered when you'd show up." I forgot how tall the devil's wing-man stood nearly seven feet.

"Good evening Edward. Time to pay the piper as they say." Mephistopheles sat in the chair next to me.

I blew smoke rings in his face and laughed. "I know all about contracts. I've practiced contract law for thirty-six years."

This seemed to amuse him. "Experience? Try hundreds of years dealing with mankind's greed and desires. You are still a rookie when it comes to contracts."

I tapped my cigar lightly onto the ashtray watching the burning ashes. "Should I turn on a light?"

"You know I have an aversion to light."

Jumping to my feet, I began switching on every lamp in the room. "Now I can see you in all your ugliness." He wore a black cape over his leathery crimson skin. Huge red wings and a bearded face with small horns completed the fallen angel's appearance. "If you made a deal with your boss Satan for good looks, you need to rescind the deal." It was my turn to laugh.

"Glad to see you are in good spirits knowing your soul is going to eternal damnation in a matter of hours. The fires of Hell are real and waiting for you." His large frame shifted uncomfortably in the chair. "Most men in your position are crying and begging. Praying to the god they betrayed for a last minute reprieve. Take me to the pearly gates. Please god please." His laughing filled the room.

"No regrets, no begging from me." I drank deeply from my Scotch rocks. "A deal is a deal. After my years of contract law cases, I know if the t's are crossed and the i's dotted, a contract is a legally binding agreement in any court of law."

Displaying the ancient book in his hands, he said, "I

Mephistopheles

brought the book you signed in blood in case you would argue that you never wrote Edward J. Sterling Jr. inside."

My laughter stopped him. "Sorry, please continue."

"A sense of humor still?" The face of evil spoke. "Your soul will be mine. You had your successful life, your wealth, your bling as they call it today."

"Yes, that was part of the contract or was it?"

"Are you trying to confuse me? Do not waste my time Edward. This is not my only stop tonight."

I left the room and refilled my Scotch. "If these are my last hours on earth," I said entering the room again, "I get to select the topic of our discussion. The other souls can wait."

"I will play along with your game for now. But do not try my patience Edward." His personality could change from charming to screaming in a second. I've witnessed both.

"I graduated from Notre Dame and remained there for my three years of law school. By my last year, I had met my future wife, Abby. We didn't know until graduation day that she was pregnant with our son, Frank."

"You are boring me," Mephistopheles commented.

"Wait till you enter the story." I puffed on my cigar before placing it in the ashtray. "When the final rank of my law school class came out, I dropped to twelfth. Sure I graduated from Notre Dame but the top ten lawyers were guaranteed the big money. This is when you came into my life."

"The star arrives." He smiled his crooked yellow teeth at me.

"I was desperate. Abby and I married. The big law firms passed me by. I had huge college loans. I had a family."

"You needed my assistance. I met you at midnight in your apartment."

A Story A Day Keeps the EVIL Away

"Then you painted the picture of golden tomorrows, of power, prestige, and wealth. At twenty-five, my mind was law school sharp. I listened to your offer. Weighed the pros and cons."

"Mankind is weak." Mephistopheles continued, "I tell people what they want to hear. Money for a soul. People are not even sure what the soul is. If only they knew! Losing one's soul did not matter when one is desperate or greedy like you."

"Have you ever lost a soul you thought was signed, sealed, not delivered?"

Mephistopheles responded, "I try not to dwell on that." He seemed to choose his words with care. "Of course over hundreds of years, someone slips away. A very rare occurrence."

I smiled at his lies. He would never admit to failure in front of a mere mortal. "Back to my story, I signed your book in blood. Edward J. Sterling Jr. The contract between us began."

"You have no regrets?"

"None for Edward J. Sterling Jr. Within a week I flew to New York and interviewed at Danford and Associates. They hired me. I made six figures by my third year at the firm. My stock choices were golden. We had more money than we could spend."

"A fairy tale came true." He answered with sarcasm. "Are we done reminiscing? I have other places to be."

"No." I finished my cigar. "Abby became famous for her charity work and served on many boards in the art world. Then came her heart attack. I called for you."

"Yes, we met a second time."

"But you wouldn't help her. My contract did not include her deteriorating health. Damn you!"

"A deal is a deal. You said it yourself." He rose from

Mephistopheles

the chair and began pacing back and forth. "The hour is late Edward."

"Frank became successful in the brokerage business selling commodities on Wall Street. He married Ava and they are expecting their first child soon."

"Enough! Let us finish our business." Mephistopheles marched towards me. His size alone intimidated and then there were those glowing eyes of fire.

"Sit down," I said as firmly as I could. "Let's talk about that contract you think you have." I smiled at the evil being.

Mephistopheles returned to his chair. "We both know your last hours on earth have changed to minutes. Ticktock, time is almost up."

"About that contract..." I teased him.

"Again?"

I stood and acted out the part of my favorite contracts law professor, Dr. Metger. Yeah, the same guy who wrote all those books and was on the short list for the Supreme Court. "Each side enters into a contract with a promise made. The first party offers a life of wealth and fame. The second party offers in return his immortal soul. A binding contract is made when, in this case, his name is signed in blood in your book of souls."

"Yes, yes. I need to leave!" His anger grew with each word.

"What if a mistake happened to void the contract?"

"Impossible!"

"Oh no, very possible." I lit my final cigar to celebrate my victory. "The name I signed in your book look at it again. Open your book of souls."

"What exactly am I looking for?" His vicious temper nearly exploded.

"The name Edward J. Sterling Jr."

A Story A Day Keeps the EVIL Away

"Yes. I see your signature. What is your point?"

I blew smoke in his direction. "That's not my name. My father was named Ralph and my grandfather Benjamin. Sorry no junior. You made a deal with someone who doesn't even exist! I keep my soul. You lose!"

His book flew past my head. He shrieked. Suddenly, the archdevil appeared to regain his composure. "You win your soul. But you gave away another's soul tonight. Remember what you did for all eternity!"

"What are you talking about? There is no Edward J. Sterling Jr."

"Call your son." Mephistopheles vanished from sight.

I dropped my cell and tried again for his number. "Frank?"

"I was just about to call you. We have great news dad. Ava had a boy and we named him after you, Edward J. Sterling Jr."

"NO! NO! NO!" I stumbled backwards, fell and left this world a broken, bitter man.

Justice For All

The Principal

Woodrow Woody Williams stared out at the snow accumulating on the sidewalk in front of Kennedy High School. Monday again. How many more Mondays till retirement? Too many! He finished the last sip of coffee and tossed the Dunkin' Donuts cup across the room, off the wall and into the wastebasket. He smiled at his small victory.

As an African American male, he thought that would give him an edge in dealing with inner city students. It didn't. Kids today didn't respect anybody, even each other, he thought. Black, white, blue, whatever color the person was wouldn't help you in this job. Being a mean son of a bitch got a better response, certainly got their attention.

A knock on his office door Mrs. Ray, his head secretary, walked in saying, "There are four teachers out today and we have three substitute teachers. But you need to talk to Miss Collins. She's demanding to see you."

A Story A Day Keeps the EVIL Away

"Thanks Mrs. Ray. Send her in." Miss Collins, a first year teacher, had the nickname Flame because of her temper and her tendency to blush when angry. A cute little blonde straight out of college, she should be teaching in the suburbs, not the city, he reflected. If he had any hair left, he would have pulled it out over her demands. No wonder the students called him Bald Eagle behind his back.

Miss Collins entered wearing a navy pantsuit with her hair pulled back into a ponytail. She carried a stack of books and dumped them on top of Williams's desk. "I QUIT! You can have my grade book, lesson plan book and all my teacher's editions. I don't need them anymore!"

"Please sit down. Let's not make a rash decision."

"I can't do another day in this hellhole!" She paced back and forth.

"Maybe you should talk to your union rep Jackie Majors." He didn't know what else to say to her. "Take the day off and get some rest. Things will look better tomorrow."

"I QUIT!" Miss Collins stormed out of his office slamming the door. Could this day get any worse?

Mr. Williams walked through the office and into the front hallway. The halls were crowded. Several groups of students stood in conversation making no effort to head for first period classes. Until his booming, gruff voice yelled, "Let's clear the halls and get to class!" Reluctantly, the groups divided disappearing into classrooms.

Suddenly two police officers appeared from an adjoining hallway followed by a mother, daughter and a female detective. The detective spoke first, "Principal Williams we need to talk to you."

"Follow me to my office." Yes, this day could get worse!

Justice For All

"What's this about?" He asked as he closed his office door behind them.

"We are here to arrest one of your teachers for the statutory rape of a student," the detective revealed.

The Teacher

Mr. Bradley Remer glanced in the mirror by the classroom door. His straw-colored hair grew long and he usually had that "need a haircut" look. But his morning runs before school kept his body long and lean. A fact he was proud of and a brag point with his fellow teachers. Remer stood outside his classroom waiting for the arrival of his senior English students. Mr. Williams expected all the teachers at their doors greeting students. The real reason to provide extra hall security, more eyes looked for potential problems. Morning coffee had forced him awake to face another week of school.

Here comes trouble, he thought, as ReRe ran into his classroom. He watched her hop on his desk kicking her brown legs in her short denim skirt and red Jordans. The bell rang. Mr. Remer called out, "ReRe go to your class. That's the bell."

"Get outta here bitch!" Sissy screamed from the back of the classroom. "Leave my teacher alone."

ReRe jumped down. "I'm not running from you! Bring your ugly ass up here!"

Mr. Remer grabbed ReRe by the arm and led her in the direction of the door. "I'll talk to you later. I don't want any confrontations in my room. Go to class ReRe."

"Yes Bradley," she laughed. ReRe hugged a security guard who escorted her down the hall.

"It's Mr. Remer," he spoke to an empty hallway.

A Story A Day Keeps the EVIL Away

Closing the door, he turned to face his students. "Okay, back to Othello. Who remembers what we read last week?"

Sissy's hand rose. "Why did you let her in your room?"

"Let's get back to Iago and the handkerchief."

"Me and the sisters can tune her up for you," Sissy added. Remer knew Sissy didn't need help from anyone else.

"Enough Sissy." Remer tried to remain calm. "Now how does Iago acquire the strawberry handkerchief?"

Two police officers entered the room with one officer reaching for his handcuffs. "Mr. Bradley Remer we are placing you under arrest." He cuffed the surprised teacher.

"Hey! What's going on here?" Remer pleaded. The classroom exploded in cell phone pictures, texts, and loud laughter.

"You're coming with us. You have the right to remain silent." As the policemen continued his Miranda rights into the hallway, students left their seats. Then Mr. Williams walked in and the students scrambled back to their desks.

"Mr. Williams why did they arrest our teacher?" A quiet boy in the front asked.

"Son, I'm sure the media will be all over this story. They love to say bad things about Kennedy High." Oh lord, he thought, will this day ever end? And it was only 8:12 a.m.

The Student

Detective Emily Rodgers sat down at the principal's desk and stared at Makia Davis. A little girl of fifteen shouldn't have to endure sexual advances from a man more than twice her age. Emily recalled losing her virginity at a college frat party. Even nineteen seemed young to her now. But fifteen was too soon. This poor girl had no idea of the media attention a trial would bring to her and her family.

Makia wore her school uniform of a red polo shirt and navy denim skirt. Her long black hair was pulled back into a silver clip. Makia wiped away her tears and gripped her mother's hand tightly. "I'm ready for your questions," her shaking voice said.

Emily smiled trying to relax the young student. "Call me Emily, Makia. Let's review some of the details from your statement."

"Is this necessary?" Mrs. Davis interrupted.

"Yes, I'm afraid so. This is a serious charge." Turning to Makia, she continued, "When and where did this incident occur?"

"Friday. On my way home from school it rained real hard. Mr. Remer stopped and offered me a ride home."

"But he didn't take you straight home."

"No. We drove to Memorial Park. He parked away from the road."

"You had sexual intercourse with Mr. Remer?"

"Yes." Makia searched her mother's face. "I'm sorry momma. It's true."

"Is this the only time you had sexual relations with Mr. Remer?"

"No. There were two other times."

"In his car too?"

"Yes. He kept a red plaid blanket on the back seat."

Detective Rodgers reviewed her notes. "Okay. All the details are exactly the same as the statement you made last night. I have two more questions then your mother can take you home."

Makia nodded fighting back more tears.

A Story A Day Keeps the EVIL Away

"How did this relationship begin with Mr. Remer?"

"He's my English teacher. Sometimes I would stay after class and help him grade papers or decorate the classroom. He bought me McDonald's a few times and I would eat lunch in his room. He said I was special. He touched me, hugged me. One time we went for a ride after school."

"Why didn't you report Mr. Remer when it happened the first time?"

Even Makia's tissue couldn't stop the tears. "He said he loved me. Nobody ever said that to me not even you momma."

Mrs. Davis pulled her from the chair and headed for the door. Detective Rodgers spoke to them, "I'll call you." But they were gone. Emily Rodgers shook her head. Why were parents always the last to know, she wondered. Picking up her purse, she walked out of the office.

The Reporter

Quinton Lancaster laughed every time he saw the framed picture of Ron Burgundy on his desk. That helped somewhat with the resentment everyone in the newsroom had for him. He dealt with being the office smart ass as well as the eldest son of legendary ABC news anchor Jerry Lancaster. Connections from his father got him his job and everyone knew it.

But the trial would change everything. A small story about a fifteen-year-old girl raped by her teacher had caught fire across the country with the media fanning the flames. A career making story had fallen into his lap that no one else wanted at first. Quinn's report with a national audience would elevate him perhaps to that NBC weekend news anchor position? At least he might get a date with Maryann, the hot anchor who all

Justice For All

the guys drooled over when she walked by. Maryann knew it and wore tight sweaters and short skirts to drive the men mad.

"Are you preparing for your update on the six o'clock news?" The deep voice of Russ Thomas, his station chief, brought him out of his daydream of Maryann.

"Yes sir. Ready to go."

"You have ten minutes till sound check. Straighten your tie. The whole country's watching. CNN might even rebroadcast your report."

Quinn remembered selecting the exact shirt, tie, and suit for this moment, his biggest moment until the trial started next week and he would be the only reporter working live with True Trial TV. He rechecked the teleprompter and took a deep breath, advice his father had shared with him. Even though he partied his way through his university days, father would get him a position with one phone call, two at the most. Friends with better voices and far more talent still searched for that first broadcasting job while he began his fifth year at station KYC.

Maryann gave her best smile saying, "Let's get an update from Quinn Lancaster on the trial of Ohio teacher Bradley Remer."

For a brief second he stared at Maryann's beautiful face and auburn hair. Then he turned to the camera and the waiting teleprompter. "Good evening. Monday begins the trial of Bradley Remer for the alleged rape of his fifteen-year-old student. Reports tell me that Bradley's wife Vicki has moved back home with her husband to present a united front for the trial. True Trial TV has signed releases from Bradley Remer and Mrs. Davis, the mother of the rape victim. Therefore, the trial will be on live TV. I will report everything to you as we watch the trial together Monday 9:00 a.m. on True Trial TV."

A Story A Day Keeps the EVIL Away

The Trial

"I'm speaking to you from outside the doors of the Franklin County Courthouse in Columbus, Ohio. Just a few moments until the trial that all of America is waiting to see. Let's have a brief comment from the parties involved. Quinn Lancaster, KYC News, Mr. Remer, what are your thoughts before the trial begins?"

"I've waited three months to clear my name. This has been very hard on myself and my wife Vicki. I want to be back in the classroom with my students. The truth will be heard today for the first time." An emotional Bradley Remer walked through the doors with his attorney.

Mrs. Davis stood in front of her daughter. "I got something to say too."

"Mrs. Davis tell America your feelings about your daughter and Mr. Remer."

"That devil needs to be locked up! He violated my Makia and robbed her of her innocence. That son of a bitch!" She stomped past the news crew dragging her daughter by the hand.

"True Trial TV reminds the audience that both the Davis and Remer families are being paid for allowing us to broadcast their trial to you. Whatever the verdict of Judge Tolliver, even if it involves a prison sentence, will be carried out like any courtroom trial. Let's go inside and watch today's True Trial."

With the cameras in position, Quinn sat down in the final row of seats. The bailiff announced, "Everyone please rise for the Honorable Judge Spencer Tolliver." A silver-haired man in a black robe entered.

He hammered his gavel. "Please be seated." Judge Tolliver

Justice For All

looked around at the crowded courtroom and the cameras, the damn cameras! "Before we begin today's proceedings, let me speak off the record about True Trial TV. I personally don't believe that the trial of a fifteen-year-old girl should be broadcast to the public. That being said, both Mr. Remer and Mrs. Davis signed legal documents allowing for this to happen. Mr. Dent for the prosecution please proceed with your opening remarks."

A veteran of True Trial TV, Dent smiled for the cameras and spoke to the judge, "Your honor, this is a horrible case of the rape of an innocent fifteen-year-old girl, Makia Davis. Mr. Remer violated the public trust of a teacher working daily with our sons and daughters. He is a rapist and needs to be sent to prison."

The judge faced the defense table. "And your opening remarks Mr. Turner."

Jake Turner, the college roommate and lifelong friend of Bradley Remer, stood in front of the judge. "Your honor, the good name of Bradley Remer has been damaged by the media for months. It ends today. You will see that we are dealing with a school girl's crush on her English teacher, a fantasy romance that is all in this little girl's imagination."

Dent announced, "I call Detective Rodgers to the stand."

"Bailiff, please swear her in."

Emily Rodgers felt the eyes of every male in the room watch her walk. Great, she thought, with all the cameras too she'll probably attract a stalker or two.

"Detective Rodgers when did you meet Makia Davis?" Dent began.

"On Sunday after the incident on Friday, Mrs. Davis brought her daughter to the police station."

A Story A Day Keeps the EVIL Away

"And what happened?"

"I took Makia's statement about being raped by Mr. Remer."

"Did you believe her story?"

"Of course! The next morning the three of us met at Kennedy High and reviewed her statement. Word for word everything was the same."

"Thank you detective. Your witness Mr. Turner."

Turner checked his notes as he approached Detective Rodgers. "Good morning detective. Just a few questions for you. You had a search warrant for my client's Buick. What did you find?"

"We were looking for a blanket that Makia described. It wasn't there."

"What else detective?"

"There were no hair fibers, DNA, nothing we could present in court."

"Thank you detective. You can return to your seat."

Dent stood frowning. "Makia Davis, please take the stand."

Makia wore her Sunday best blue dress with navy ribbons tying back her hair. She gripped several tissues in her right hand.

"Makia, you are a sophomore at Kennedy High School. How did you meet Mr. Remer?"

"He's my English teacher."

"Okay Makia, let's focus on the Friday incident. Please tell us what happened in your own words."

She hesitated searching for her mother's face in the crowd. Her mother smiled at her. Then Makia spoke, "I was walking home from school. It was raining. Mr. Remer stopped his car and offered me a ride home. I got in his car. We drove to

Justice For All

Memorial Park and that's where we did it."

"You had sexual intercourse with Mr. Remer?"

"Yes, but I wanted to like the other times."

"Other times?"

"We did it twice before that. I love Mr. Remer and he loves me. I didn't wanna go to the police. That was momma's idea."

Vicki Remer erupted in tears rushing out of the courtroom.

"No further questions. Mr. Turner?"

Turner asked, "One question Makia. Were you a virgin when this alleged affair began?"

"Objection your honor!" Dent said jumping to his feet.

Judge Tolliver responded, "I'll allow it. We have signed releases to include everything. Makia, answer the question."

Tears rolled down her cheeks as she admitted, "No, I lost my virginity to Franklin, a older boy lives on Decker, when momma was at work."

"No further questions." Turner returned to the defense table giving Bradley a thumbs up.

Dent said from his chair. "The prosecution rests."

Turner announced, "I call Principal Williams for the defense."

Williams checked his watch. Homeroom would be starting in a few minutes for his Kennedy's students.

"Principal Williams, tell us about Bradley Remer."

"I've known Mr. Remer for the past six years as an English teacher at Kennedy High. He seems to be well liked by the staff and students. Several teachers are in the courtroom today. His classroom is organized and he never misses school, a model teacher."

"Thank you Principal Williams. Mr. Dent?"

"No questions."

A Story A Day Keeps the EVIL Away

"I call Bradley Remer to the stand."

The courtroom seemed to come alive with renewed interest in the trial. Remer sat down waiting for his attorney's questions.

"Mr. Remer, let's return to the Friday in question. Tell us in your own words what happened."

"I was driving home and saw my student, Makia Davis, walking in the pouring rain. I stopped my car and gave her a ride home."

"That's all that happened?"

"Yes."

"Why do you believe Makia Davis would make up this story of rape?"

Bradley Remer looked past his attorney to the little girl seated next to Prosecutor Dent. "Students have crushes on their teachers. It happens all the time. In Makia's case she loves to write fantasy stories. I guess she wanted a relationship, wanted attention."

"Thank you. Mr. Dent?"

Dent's face grew angry. "Why did you rape a fifteen-year-old girl?"

"It never happened, only in her imagination. I'm happily married Mr. Dent."

"Closing remarks," Judge Tolliver instructed. Remer passed Dent as he returned to the defense table.

"Your honor, this man is a rapist and needs to be in prison. You heard Makia Davis. She was caught up in his lies, trading a promise of love for statutory rape. Send him to prison your honor."

Turner approached the judge. "There is no evidence, no witnesses. You have the words of a young girl with a vivid

Justice For All

imagination versus a family man, a teacher. Let's end this nonsense and return Mr. Remer to his classroom."

Judge Tolliver stared into the camera. "I know True Trial TV has time restraints but I am ready to rule. I find Mr. Remer innocent of all charges. Court dismissed." He hammered down the gavel for the final time.

"THIS ISN'T JUSTICE!" Mrs. Davis screamed. "MY DAUGHTER WAS RAPED!" The bailiff ran to her and escorted her out of the courtroom.

Within minutes, only Bradley Remer and his attorney remained. "That was too close Jake. Guess I better be more careful with the next girl. I got my new candidate already, her name's ReRe."

"I don't want to know Brad," Turner interrupted closing his attache case. "You're lucky the last girl took cash to keep her mouth shut."

"You know what they say, once you go black..."

"Brad, I'll call you. Maybe have lunch on the weekend. Watch yourself. Next time I won't be able to keep you outta prison."

"This is Quinn Lancaster reporting from outside the courthouse. Thanks for tuning into True Trial TV."

A Story A Day Keeps the EVIL Away

When The Rains Fell

The roar of the motorcycle zooming up the driveway and into the garage woke Keri. Again! Damn drunk of a brother-in-law! She didn't need to look at the clock. It would be after two when the bars closed on Friday nights. She hurried to lodge the kitchen chair against the locked door of her bedroom. If Keri failed to act, good old drunk Richard would "accidentally" jump into bed with her. She stood by the door listening to Richard stumble and bumble his way in the house. As she turned back to her bed, loud pounding began on the bedroom door startling her.

"KERI LET ME IN!"

"Go to your own room. Richard you're drunk."

The banging continued. "Come on Keri. How 'bout a good night kiss?"

"I'm not your wife! Sleep it off and keep your hands off my sister!" She heard Richard rush into the bathroom probably vomiting. Then she pictured his large body bouncing off the walls and falling onto his own bed passed out till morning. Keri removed the chair and unlocked the door. It would be safe now.

A Story A Day Keeps the EVIL Away

When she opened the door, she spied a light on. More than likely her sister Liz. She loved her sister but Liz always played the victim never standing up for herself.

"Liz, you're still up? It's nearly three a.m."

"Get a glass from the kitchen and have some sparkling red wine." She took a long drink waiting for her sister to join her in the family room. "I'll pour." Her hands were shaking. "Guess you should pour Keri."

Keri regarded her sister. If not for Liz's short black hair, they could pass for twins. Liz's watery green eyes stared back at Keri. "Is that a fresh bruise by your eye?"

"Yes." Liz admitted.

"You can't live like this. Leave Richard."

"And go where? I have no money. Our parents have been gone over six years. Should I live in a shelter?"

"We could leave together. I"ll help you." Keri wore her long black hair in a single braid down her back. About three years younger than Liz, Keri remained the practical sister. "Jim isn't coming back. I'm free to do what I want."

"I'm sorry Jim walked out on you." She produced a Kleenex from the pocket of her pink robe and dabbed her eyes.

"Left in the middle of the night and he never came back. That asshole!" Keri sipped her wine then sat her glass on the coffee table. "When the bank foreclosed, I lost the house. I couldn't afford the payments by myself."

"We took you in. I'm not having my sister sleeping under a bridge or in a homeless shelter."

"I appreciate that sis. I've worn out my welcome. I need to leave. Richard hates me. And I'm scared to be around him."

Liz said, "I used to love Rich. We never had kids. I think he's blamed me for that." She couldn't stop the tears from

When The Rains Fell

flowing. "How did everything turn to shit?"

Keri threw her arms around Liz. "I'm here for you. There's got to be a better life than this." They sat quietly hugging for what seemed like hours but it lasted only minutes. Finally Keri spoke, "Let's get some sleep. I'll think of something. Good night sis."

A loud buzzing sound, Rich reached for his cell on the nightstand. "What time is it? Seven thirty? Frank why are you calling so early? Raining? Didn't even watch a weather forecast last night. They're wrong most times. All day rain? There goes our golf outing. You call the other guys? Well thanks for telling me. I'm going back to sleep."

"Who called?" Liz asked. She heard the rain hitting the roof.

"Frank. No golf today. Damn, I counted on drinking and golfing all day. Why don't you take a shower and make me some breakfast?" Rich closed his eyes.

Liz couldn't sleep so she grabbed her robe and headed for the shower. Whatever happened to the mornings when Rich wouldn't let her get out of bed or when he would join her in the shower? She tried hard not to cry again. Liz let him sleep as long as possible, less hours together the better. He must have gained fifty pounds in their twelve years of marriage, she thought shaking her head. "Rich, ten minutes till breakfast if you wanna get a shower."

Rich mumbled something and walked down the short hallway to the bathroom. Within minutes he threw on his old black jeans and black Harley Davidson sleeveless t-shirt. He towel dried his short brown hair tossing the towel on the bathroom floor.

Liz brought a plate of bacon, fried eggs and toast to the

A Story A Day Keeps the EVIL Away

kitchen table. She poured his cup of black coffee. "Not shaving today?"

"Why bother? Not going anywhere but the garage. Guess I'll work on my bike."

Liz sat at the table watching him eat. She drank the remainder of her orange juice.

"You should drink coffee," Rich said as he chewed his bacon.

"We've had this discussion too many times. I just don't like the taste of it. Besides, there's more for you," she reasoned.

"Your tramp sister drinks it too. When's she moving out? No wonder Jim ran out on her! And we're not getting any rent from her, that lazy bitch!"

"Don't call her that!"

"Watch it Liz. Don't raise your voice to me! I don't wanna hit you."

"I'm sorry Rich." She pushed in her chair. Thunder crashed through the sky and the rain poured down even harder. "I'm waking Keri before I sort laundry downstairs."

Rich finished his coffee and carried his dishes to the sink. One last thing for her to bitch about leaving stuff on the table, he thought. Liz walked past him on the way to the basement, any reason to get away from Rich. He heard the shower, Keri.

A simple twist of the doorknob, Rich entered the bathroom. He pulled back the shower door reaching through the hot water and steam. His hand grabbed Keri's ass.

"What are you doing?" Keri raised her voice pulling away. "I locked that door."

"And I have the key."

"You son of a bitch! Why are you here?"

"Admiring the view Keri. You know we could hook up

When The Rains Fell

again. Pretty sweet last time."

"I was drunk. I didn't know what I was doing."

"Think 'bout it. Your sister's a coldhearted bitch but you're as hot as a firecracker on the fourth of July." He laughed closing the shower door. "I'll be in the garage if you change your mind. Liz never goes out there."

Keri dressed in jean shorts and a blue patterned blouse. She reached the kitchen finding a blueberry muffin for breakfast. When she heard the washing machine start, she hurried to the kitchen counter before Liz returned. She poured the remainder of the hot coffee in the Packers travel mug, Rich's favorite. "I'll be right back," she told Liz as she passed her in the kitchen.

Rich enjoyed spending time by himself in the garage, an attached garage so he didn't have to deal with the pouring rain. He cranked up his XM radio to classic Rolling Stones. He turned to his Harley. His motorcycle cost a lot of money still worth every penny. He began wiping off his bike when the side door opened.

Keri entered the garage. She wore her dark hair straight down her back instead of the usual long braid.

"Change your mind Keri?" Rich hoped for a positive response.

"We don't have much time." Keri handed him the Packers mug. "You can drink the rest of the coffee. I'll put on a show you'll never forget."

Rich grinned and drank the hot coffee. True to her word, Keri swayed her hips to the music and started to unbutton her blouse. Rich gulped down the final drops of coffee. Something hit him hard. His stomach exploded and white foam came out of his mouth. He took two steps towards Keri. What did that bitch do to me? He fell straight down dead.

25

A Story A Day Keeps the EVIL Away

Keri knelt down holding her hand by his neck. No pulse as she expected. Blood spilled from his smashed face that landed on the hard concrete floor. Time to tell Liz the good news. She clicked off the loud music remembering to rebutton her blouse as she left the garage.

"You need to come with me to the garage," Keri said.

"Can it wait?" Liz asked.

"No." Keri held Liz's hand and walked her out to the garage.

"OH MY GOD!" Liz screamed. "CALL 911!" Blood mixed with the white foam around Rich's head.

"We can't call 911. Calm down."

"What do you mean we can't?"

"I poisoned him. I spiked his coffee."

"YOU KILLED HIM?" Liz yelled.

Keri slapped her across the face. "He needed to die. Let's clean up. Put that coffee mug in the dishwasher. I'll take the shower curtain to wrap him in."

"We're going to jail!"

"SHUT UP!" Keri demanded. "No we're not. Give me your cell phone. I don't want you doing anything stupid." Liz surrendered her cell. "We'll get rid of his body when it gets dark. We need a story to explain Rich's disappearance."

Liz's shaking hand picked up the Packers mug and returned to the kitchen. Keri passed her carrying the shower curtain. She would have to do all the work. Liz wouldn't be mentally ready to be much help.

Placing the shower curtain on the concrete floor, it took all of Keri's strength to roll Rich over onto the plastic. An occasional salad would have helped Rich! The next step involved cleaning the blood off the floor. She searched the garage and

When The Rains Fell

the basement until she found a bottle of bleach and a scrub brush. Then Keri had to force Liz to help lift Rich's body into the back of the white SUV.

Nobody ate lunch. And dinner seemed in doubt too. Liz would burst into tears until she agreed with Keri to lay down for a very restless nap.

Keri watched it rain. The new normal seemed to be settling in. No more Richard. The house belonged to Liz and Keri. But they needed a cover story. What could they say to Rich's friends and co-workers? At least it was Saturday. Monday and his job would be here soon enough.

Suddenly a car pulled in the driveway. A man walked to the front door. Keri jumped into action when the doorbell rang.

"I'm Frank," said the tall blond-haired man in a green raincoat. "Can I talk to Rich?"

Liz paused sorting through a series of lies to tell then selected one. "I'm sorry to tell you—Rich and Liz separated. I don't know where he is."

"How about Liz? Is she home?" Frank continued.

"Yes, but she's napping. As you would expect, she's very upset. Now is not a good time. Sorry."

"Well tell Rich I stopped by. No real surprise they split up. I kinda saw it coming." He returned to his car. Keri watched him leave through the sheets of pouring rain.

Night enveloped the sky and the rain continued to fall. Keri greeted her sleepy sister with a tray of hot tea, toast and a Valium. "This will make you feel better Liz."

"Is Rich really dead or did I have a nightmare?"

"He's dead." Keri replied coldly. "Get over it. It's for your own good. Eat up. We need to leave soon. Wear old clothes and boots."

A Story A Day Keeps the EVIL Away

Keri had changed so she threw two shovels in the SUV and backed it out of the garage. Finally Liz left the house carrying her purse. Wordlessly, she sat next to Keri.

"I'll drive. I know where I'm going," Keri said trying to reassure her sister.

After several minutes Liz couldn't control the panic in her voice, "What if the police stop us? We have Rich's dead body in the car!"

"The police won't bother us," Keri replied calmly. "I'm driving the speed limit. Cops don't wanna step out in the rain if they can stay in a warm, dry police car."

"I feel sick to my stomach. This was a mistake. You shouldn't have killed him Keri."

Keri slammed on the brakes pulling to the side of the road. "SHUT UP LIZ! Did you forget about all the times he hit you? Someday you'll realize that your little sis gave you a new life!" Then she jerked the SUV back on the road.

Liz sat and stared at the wipers fighting the losing battle to keep the rain off the windshield. She fought back tears. Maybe I'll wake up in my own bed next to a snoring Richard, she thought. Suddenly she blurted out, "How do you know where to get rid of a dead body?"

Keri looked straight ahead. "It doesn't matter how I know. I just know where to go."

"Have you done this before? Kill someone?"

"Be quiet sis. Don't make me angry!"

Silence fell again. The drive continued through the rain. Keri slowly turned at the Granger National Park sign. Minutes passed as she navigated the dark roads illuminated only by the SUV headlights. She drove off the paved road following a dirt road for several more miles.

When The Rains Fell

The SUV stopped. Keri reached for the two shovels. "Come on. We have work to do." She led Liz to a small grove of trees and started shoveling. "Help me Liz. I can't do all the digging."

Liz reluctantly joined in. She cried freely only the rain washed away her tears.

"Be happy it rained all day. It's a lot easier to dig in the mud." Keri seemed to be doing twice the work but decided not to say anything. At least Liz helped.

More time passed as the digging continued. Suddenly, Liz screamed out,"There's another body down there!"

"That would be Jim."

"My god Keri! You killed him too!"

"Shut up Liz!"

"We grew up in the same house with the same parents. How could you turn into a cold blooded killer?"

"That's enough sis!"

"I'm calling the police! Give me my cell back. You're sick you need help Keri."

"You're not calling the police!" Keri raised her shovel over her head. "There's room for three bodies down there!" She slammed the shovel onto Liz's head striking her again and again.

She shoved Liz's lifeless body into the large hole. "You wanna spend forever with Richard? You got your wish Liz." Dragging, pushing Rich's body from the SUV, Keri was exhausted. But she found the strength to shovel all the dirt onto her new victims' bodies.

Keri's mind considered the new situation. She laughed out loud. Of course it would work. The drive seemed faster this time. She grabbed Liz's purse and entered the house.

A hot shower is just what the doctor ordered. Once the

A Story A Day Keeps the EVIL Away

steam cleared, Keri found the scissors in the drawer. She leaned Liz's picture on the bathroom mirror. In a way, she would miss her long hair. Her newly cut hair covered the sink. Keri smiled at her work.

The pile of her muddy clothes including the boots filled a trash bag. Keri raided Liz's clothes closet. Liz's clothes fit her, not as tight as her usual wardrobe. Next, her handwriting had to be perfect. Keri practiced repeatedly as she sat in her new family room. At last Keri looked at her reflection in the mirror saying, "Hello, my name is Liz."

If the Shoe Fits

Annie marched down the sidewalk, passed the car-lined street, and blended in with the large group of people walking towards the mansion. At that moment she searched through the crowd. "Ricky?"

"I'm here." A reluctant Ricky responded. "Told ya I'd rather wait in the car." Her flowing red hair and captivating smile made it hard for him to say no.

"This is where Vito the Mauler Lepinski lived! One of the most famous mobsters of all time. Don't you wanna see his house?" They walked through the imposing iron gate.

He caught up with her. "No. Not interested in a giant garage sale."

"It's an estate sale, not a garage sale. They're selling everything for cheap. Maybe you'll find something to buy."

"I doubt it," he said. "All the good stuff is probably gone by now. Okay, I'll play along. After all I'm Italian too."

A long table was set up opposite the front doors and had become the place of business. Two serious-looking men in short sleeve shirts sat in front of a cash box with a stack of papers

A Story A Day Keeps the EVIL Away

between them. A uniformed policeman paced behind them reflecting on his luck at getting this off duty assignment. The short line of people carried everything from lamps to paintings over to the table.

Annie grabbed Ricky's hand. "Let's explore the upstairs. There's over a dozen bedrooms."

"How exciting," Ricky yawned.

The large staircase led them to spacious hallways. After ducking in and out of several rooms, Ricky spied a king sized bed and sat down. "I'll wait for you here. At least this bed's comfortable."

"This is Vito's bedroom!"

"It's as big as the entire first floor of our house! Look a mirror on the ceiling too. Who needs a room this size?"

Annie pointed at the burgundy couch and chairs with the well-stocked bar. "Bet a lotta deals went down here. Probably gave orders to have people killed."

"You read too much. That's gossip not fact. I heard he never served a day in jail."

"Gangsters got the best lawyers. Everyone knows that."

Ricky reached under the bed. "Hey look what I found—black patent leather shoes! I could use new dress shoes. I'm sure they won't fit." Ricky tried on both shoes and stood up. "Damn, they actually fit. Good condition too. I'm guessing two hundred easy for these."

Annie entered the huge walk-in closet. "There's still some of his suits in here. Maybe you can find a suit to go with your shoes."

"Thought he was fat."

Annie laughed. "You haven't looked in the mirror lately."

He flipped through the suits and pulled out a black three-

If the Shoe Fits

piece suit. "What'd think Annie?"

"You'll fit in at Muraski's Funeral Home." She placed a black felt hat on his head. "Now you look like a real gangster!"

They cut short the rest of their upstairs tour and joined the line of customers. "Don't know what they'll charge me." Ricky remembered having about a hundred and twenty in his wallet and had to buy dinner tonight for them. "I wonder if Vito left me some cash." He laughed this time.

Ricky rifled through the suit pockets and retrieved a handful of hundred dollar bills. Since the line was slow, he counted out twelve hundred dollars. This day just kept getting better! "I owe you a special dinner tonight honey." He flashed the roll of hundreds for only her to see.

"Wow!" Annie reacted. "Let's dress up for dinner. You can wear your new clothes."

They reached the table with the emotionless men staring at them. "What are you buying?" The man on the left asked.

"Gotta suit, shoes and oh yeah this hat."

The second man wrote everything on a blank sheet of paper. "Your offer?"

"Two hundred for everything?"

"Done. Sign here and put today's date. All sales are final, no refunds."

Annie left the mansion and began strolling through the colorful flower gardens, neatly trimmed hedges and Roman style water fountains. Ricky followed closely behind. He would not complain this time. Maybe he finally got lucky; his ship had come in at last.

Hours later, they dressed for their night on the town. "Yes you need to wear a tie Ricky." She stood in her white slip staring into her closet. Something dressy, something sexy. The short

A Story A Day Keeps the EVIL Away

navy dress always looked good showing off just enough of her shapely figure to turn a few heads when she entered a room. Of course she would add the pearl necklace.

Ricky walked in with two ties. "The blue stripes or the solid red?"

"Blue, it'll match my dress." She was startled by his smack on her behind as he left the room. "You'll pay for that Ricky." She giggled.

"I plan on collecting babe." He called to her. "How 'bout that expensive Italian place, the Golden Bowl?"

"You need reservations to eat there."

"Well let's stop anyhow. I should buy a lottery ticket with my luck today." As he zipped her dress, he said, "You look amazing!"

"And you look like a gangster out of the old black-and-white movies, especially with that hat."

After a short drive, they reached the Golden Bowl. Annie took his arm as they walked up to the maître d'. "Need a table for two Oscar." Ricky said to the white coated man.

"Vito?" Oscar couldn't hide the shocked look on his face. "Of course, your usual table follow me." He tried to regain his composure.

They sat at a small table by the enormous fireplace. The waiter appeared handing them menus and pouring glasses of water.

"Tony, how's the veal tonight?"

"Delicious, your favorite meal I know. Sorry for giving you menus Mr. Lepinski. A pleasure to have you dining with us again." Tony reached for the menus and disappeared into the kitchen.

"How do you know everyone's names?" Annie questioned.

If the Shoe Fits

"I thought you never ate here before."

"They wear name tags I guess."

"No, they don't Ricky."

Ricky shook his head. "Can't tell you. It just came to me."

Tony returned and filled their wine glasses with champagne. Then he left the bottle in a bucket of ice by Ricky's chair.

"You'll love the veal doll. Best I ever had!"

Annie said,"Ricky, you're doing it again! You're scaring me. It's like you became Vito!"

"Don't be silly." He grabbed her leg under the table. "Who else would do that?"

"Okay, I'm overreacting. Let's enjoy our dinner."

The salad bowls were quickly joined by their dinner plates of veal and penne. They ate quietly. Ricky refilled their glasses until the bottle was empty.

Oscar rapidly crossed the restaurant to Ricky's table. "Vito, you need to leave now! The Torelli brothers pulled up in a white limo. Follow me through the kitchen. We have a car waiting for you."

"Annie, we gotta scram. Those are the Torelli brothers who killed me!"

Too startled to talk, Annie's wine glass slipped from her hand spilling champagne on the white tablecloth. She took Ricky's hand. It felt like a dream or a nightmare and she couldn't wake up. They rushed past the kitchen crew and into the dark sedan in the alley.

Oscar closed the car door. "That was too close," he said to the darkening night sky.

"Is it really you Vito?" The driver asked as he drove rapidly through the downtown streets.

"Michael, good to have you at the wheel. Like old times."

A Story A Day Keeps the EVIL Away

Was it the champagne? Had she fallen asleep watching Edward G. Robinson in a gangster movie? Tell me this can't be happening; Annie cried into her hands.

"Change of plans tonight Michael. Drop us off at 1370 Wallings. Then disappear. I'll see you in the morning, usual time."

"Whatever you say boss. Gotta a little hideaway for you and the girl. Fine by me."

Annie waited in her lace robe until she heard Ricky snoring. As she expected, he piled all of his clothes on the bedroom floor. Whatever spell Ricky was under, the clothes appeared to be the key. She scooped them up, with his shoes, into a garbage bag and threw it in the trash can behind the garage. Perhaps she could sleep and life would be normal in the morning.

Ricky emerged from the shower towel-drying his black hair. "Annie, I barely remember what happened last night. I should never drink champagne."

Putting on her robe again, she responded, "We had a great time, especially when we got home."

"That I remember!" He smiled when the sizzling memory resurfaced. "You're incredible."

Annie kissed his cheek. "I'll make some coffee while you get dressed."

Ricky called out to her, "Hey, where's my new suit?"

She didn't answer. Maybe the genie was finally back in the bottle. No more mobster Vito.

"I found my new shoes. Must've put them in the closet."

Shoes, Annie thought, they were tossed away too. She poured the water in the coffeemaker and flipped the switch.

Ricky appeared in all of his gangster clothes—black suit, black shoes and hat. Annie was speechless. No, it couldn't be

If the Shoe Fits

possible! "Ricky?"

"Who's Ricky?"

Ricky/Vito kissed her hard on the lips and squeezed her ass. "Thanks for last night doll. I feel like a new man. See you soon. Michael's got your address." Then he walked out the door and into the waiting Lincoln Town Car.

Annie collapsed onto the kitchen chair in a burst of tears. Why? Why was this happening?

"Where to boss?" Michael asked.

"Silvio's. Gotta connect with the boys. Let 'em know I'm back."

"Oscar called me from the restaurant. Said the Torelli brothers came in heavy looking to kill you. Guess they went away disappointed." Michael finished the drive and opened the car door. "Call me when you're ready to leave boss."

Ricky walked through the side door of Silvio's. "Hey Frankie, good to see ya."

Frankie's large frame slowly rose from the desk chair. Stacks of twenties, fifties, and hundreds covered the desk. "Vito?"

"Who else?" He hugged Frankie patting him on the back. "How'd we do last night?"

"Pretty good. I'm still counting. Surprised to see you Vito." Shocked better described his true feelings as he returned to his chair.

"We need to hit Dominic and Vinnie Torelli. They were gunning for me at the Golden Bowl. We gotta put them in the ground."

"Lemme call Max. His crew would be perfect. Nobody knows them." Frankie dialed and nodded to Vito. "They'll be here in ten minutes."

A Story A Day Keeps the EVIL Away

"I'm going too."

"Not a good idea Vito. They'll see you coming."

"I'll stay outta sight. I gotta watch them die for what they did to me!"

Joey, a slender man in his twenties, walked in. "Rumors must be true! Vito lemme make you a drink. Scotch and water?"

"Always, thanks Joey. Good to be back." Ricky sipped his Scotch and waited.

The phone rang. "Yea," Frankie answered. "Keep an eye on 'em. Call me here if they leave." Frankie hung up the phone and wrote on a small piece of paper. "Got an address, Hillcrest Motel over on State. The Torellis are staying there."

Max opened the door. His blonde hair and glasses reminded Ricky that he wasn't Italian but had proven his loyalty many times. A ruthless killer he could rely on.

"Here's the address." Ricky handed him the paper. "I'm riding along with you."

"Yes Mr. Lepinski. Whenever you're ready."

Max opened the back door of the black Impala for Ricky. Two other men were already seated rechecking the clips from their pistols. Max took the wheel as they slowly approached Hillcrest Motel. He stopped and gave the orders. "Front door for you two. Bobby take the parking lot. I'll take the door."

Like a smooth military operation, Max's boot kicked open the motel door. All three men fired before the Torellis could reach their guns. Dominic never got off the bed. Vinnie fell by the bathroom door riddled in bullets. Max shot each brother in the head.

Ricky stood by the motel door. "Good job! I could always count on you Max." Then he turned and walked away.

Frankie answered the ringing phone. "Max, is it done?"

If the Shoe Fits

"Yes. You won't believe this Frankie. Vito vanished. All we found was a pile of his clothes. Can't find him anywhere."

"Is this a joke? It ain't funny Max."

Annie started to calm down by her second cup of coffee. Nothing made any sense. Vito back from the dead? Suddenly Ricky walked in the house. Annie jumped up and greeted him with a big hug. "I'm really glad to see you."

"Crazy thing is I don't have any shoes." A confused Ricky added, "And I'm standing here without any pants on. What's been going on?"

A Story A Day Keeps the EVIL Away

Jesse's Story

feeling real weak...sick...taste of vomit in my mouth...can't trust no one here...gotta find a place by myself...shadows from the bridge...getting dark, cold...winter coming...don't matter only the needle...escape feel good again...they're watching me...take anything from you...lost my blanket one night...gotta place to fix...need it NOW...white, brown powder don't matter...hands shaking...lighter, spoon...ready...find a vein...shoot that sweet H into my arm...everything's slowing down...mellow, relaxed, peaceful...drowsy...wasn't always like this...a lost soul living under a bridge...had a life, have memories...keep forgetting more and more of my other life...

Name's Jesse James Lewis glad to meet ya. Hide the women and lock the liquor cabinets! Just kidding. I got stories for you about my favorite topic—me! Don't know why you'd want to hear 'em but here goes.

Guess my parents had a sense of humor calling me Jesse James. I'm Jess to my friends. Life was kinda drifting along till my best friend Kenny told me to meet him after school. We walked down to the railroad tracks. Kenny lit up a cigarette and

A Story A Day Keeps the EVIL Away

offered me one. My first smoke at age twelve.

I coughed when I inhaled. Kenny laughed. Then I got the hang of it and had my second cigarette. Pretty soon I began stealing a pack of cigarettes out of mom's hiding place. Me and Kenny began smoking nearly every day after school.

Mom never asked about the missing cigarettes. I must've smelled like smoke every night when I came home. But she had her own problems with dad walking out on us. Sometimes she would leave the dinner table in tears. Smoking was the last thing on her mind.

On my fourteenth birthday Kenny said, "Jess meet me by the tracks. Got a surprise for you." I gobbled down my dinner. Didn't need a story for mom 'cause it was summer. And my birthday.

Kenny waited for me with a six-pack of beer. My first beer ever tasted bitter. His older brother Dick joined us. He started high school last year so he hooked us up for the beer. Never liked the taste of beer. They drank. I drank. You get used to it after awhile. Occasionally their brother Randy would show up to smoke with us if he could pry himself away from Jill, the first girl at our school to develop curves. Randy and Jill stayed a couple through high school.

Beer and cigarettes made me feel like an adult. Good enough for junior high. But when I entered Roosevelt High School, everyone seemed more worldly than me. "You haven't smoked pot?" Kids would laugh at me. Before I asked Kenny, he already had a fresh supply of marijuana for me and the other guys.

Down by our usual hideout by the tracks, I lit up my first joint. It looked like a funny cigarette. I got high and felt mellow. The other guys watched me amused. I noticed a real hunger

Jesse's Story

afterwards. Dick pulled small bags of chips from his backpack tossing one in my direction. Smoking pot became a regular activity, not in school though. Dick got busted in the restroom for smoking pot and suspended for a whole week. We waited till school ended every day and met by the tracks.

Dating was new for me. I felt awkward around girls. I doubled with Randy and dated Jill's sister, Carla. A big night for me would be talking to Carla and a kiss at the end of the night. Of course we had to wait till Randy and Jill finished in the back seat of his car.

I never noticed the attention I got from the females at our school as I "filled out," not the skinny white boy anymore. Enter Mrs. Keri Kent, my social studies teacher in my junior year and by far the most attractive teacher at our school. I had her class at the end of the day. She asked me, "Jess, can you stay after and help move some boxes?"

Again, I didn't react to her staring at me until the second time, until she touched my face. She closed the closet door behind her and gave me my first real kiss. "Can you come home with me?" I could feel the heat radiating from her.

Hell yes I rode home with her! "Call me Keri but not at school okay?" At this point I would agree to anything. "Duck down in your seat I don't want the neighbors to talk." She took the clip out of her blonde hair and it fell to her shoulders. We pulled in the garage. Keri led me to her bedroom and removed two joints from a dresser drawer. She lighted candles everywhere in the room.

"Wow! This is the strongest pot I've ever smoked!" I said as she undressed both of us. The next few hours I'll never forget. The saying goes you learn something every day. I learned a lot that afternoon.

43

A Story A Day Keeps the EVIL Away

When I arrived at her class the next day, she gave me a quick smile. But that was all. Did I do something wrong? Was it because I didn't know what to do in the bedroom? I ruined everything. That lasted for over a week.

"Jess, can I speak to you after class?" She wore a short navy dress with gold buttons that I couldn't take my eyes off. I pictured her in bed with me. We didn't speak until we were riding in her car. "Sorry, I had to wait until my husband's working late. I've missed you Jess."

I put my hand on her leg while she drove. Then we were in her bedroom and I smelled the lit scented candles. She pulled back the covers on her bed when I asked, "Can I have some pot?" I enjoyed the high from the joint we shared as much as the high from her body. After smoking, this time I felt more in control, not a rookie anymore. We fell asleep briefly. I heard the garage door open.

"Oh my god! Brian's home. Get out! Get out!" She screamed.

I pulled on my boxers, grabbed my clothes off the floor and jumped out the bedroom window. I'll never know what happened between Keri and her husband Brian that night. She wasn't at school for the next two days. When she showed up on Friday, even her makeup couldn't cover the bruise on her right cheek. We never spoke again although I did get straight A's in her class. Extra credit rules!

Keri Kent ruined me for high school girls. Experience matters. Teenage girls weren't worth the effort. I went back to smoking more pot. Kenny found the stronger stuff that Keri gave me.

Nothing in life is free except advice. The new pot proved to be very expensive. Kenny and Dick introduced me to a money

Jesse's Story

making venture, garage shopping. You drive out of town where nobody knows you. Then you look for open garages late at night, like two to four a.m. You steal anything you can sell. Kenny's connections helped fence: skis, snow blowers, mowers, GPS devices, anything of value.

That one night we almost got caught. I'm dragging these heavy snow skis out of the garage. The house lights came on and some mad dude in sweatpants flew out the back door. Dick took one of the skis and swung it head high at the charging man. Knocked him on his ass! We laughed all the way to Kenny's car.

Smoking pot under the bleachers while the Roosevelt Raiders lost another football game, memories like that stick with you. But it was time for me to graduate and go to college. Mom couldn't hide her happiness and amazement that a college would accept me. Things changed for all of us. Dick's parents signed him into drug rehab. Randy and Jill got married the summer after we graduated. Their baby arrived by the fall. We were surprised it hadn't happened sooner knowing their nightly activities.

Kenny and I headed to Edison State University together. It didn't take long for Kenny to find the campus drug dealers. We had access to crack cocaine and molly too. The next problem was how to pay for our drugs. No garages to raid on a college campus. We adjusted to life in the dorms. The reefer smell filled the air on weekends. Laptops, TVs, even cash waited for us to steal. That worked for awhile. Only Kenny wanted to steal cars too. He started hot wiring a Ford truck one day. I sat inside with him yelling,"Hurry up Kenny! Hurry up!"

Bruce Gelman, the dorm resident, came running out screaming into his cell,"CAMPUS POLICE! CAMPUS POLICE!" It was his truck! We agreed to leave Edison U. and no charges

45

A Story A Day Keeps the EVIL Away

would be filed. I bet the campus crime wave ended too.

Back home with mom, I bounced from job to job. I made enough to pay for my drug habit. Kenny became a full-time drug dealer. No surprise there. I needed a regular job so I could give mom some money and help her out. Mom talked to Randy and Kenny's mother. Suddenly I'm getting a call from Randy who had early success in the insurance business. He sponsored me at United Insurance. I attended the classes and tested for my state licenses.

I knew I had to cut back on the drugs that now included pot and crack cocaine. A lot harder than I thought. Withdrawal's a bitch! The urge to get high was overwhelming. Everybody around me used too, not any positive support from them. I would find myself thinking about drugs all day long, even in the middle of the night. Nothing got me high anymore. Maybe I needed something stronger.

Within six months, Randy got his own office and left the cubicles. A few weeks after that, I did too. My own office! I had nothing to hang on the walls except my state insurance licenses framed. I chose the bottom desk drawer for my stash and found a way to lock it.

Randy walked in to see my new office. "It's almost as large as mine." He admitted to me, "I'm totally off drugs."

"Good for you Randy. I've been cutting back."

"But I'm worried about Jill. I think she's still using. She sneaks around so I won't catch her. Maybe you can help her. She won't listen to me. Let me set something up for the two of you to talk."

"Sure Randy. Any way I can help. You've done so much for me."

I don't remember what came first. Either my fatal meeting

Jesse's Story

with Kenny and my new drug or lunch with Jill that became so much more.

"Kenny, I can't get high anymore. You got something stronger, a real rush?"

Welcome to the wonderful world of heroin! "You need to try horse."

"Isn't that heroin? I can't put a needle in my arm. Got this thing about needles."

We were down by the tracks, first time in a long time. "You can smoke it like pot or crack. Try it."

I lit up waiting to be taken away on a magic carpet ride. I didn't wait long. I collapsed on the ground feeling wonderful, happy and high. My troubles were gone. It must have been hours later when it finally ended. "Sign me up Kenny. You were right!"

Randy made lunch reservations for Jill and me, even paid for it. Since she was Randy's wife, I never looked at her that way. Jill dressed in a low cut yellow sweater and black skirt. I had feelings for her before the waitress took our order.

"Guess Randy wants you off drugs." I began trying not to stare into those crystal blue eyes.

"I like getting high. Can't stop myself. Not in front of Randy though. You use don't you Jess?" She asked.

"Yea. Maybe we could get high together." I got lost in her eyes. Short black hair framed her pretty face. We both stood up at the same time passing our waitress bringing drinks to our table. Some things can't wait. One of those cheap motels over by the interstate seemed perfect for us. I brought the strong pot into the motel room. We smoked and then fell very relaxed into bed. Quite a lunch and Randy paid for the room!

I avoided Randy at the office the next day. But he knocked

47

A Story A Day Keeps the EVIL Away

on my office door and walked in. "Jess, you're a miracle worker! She's happy, said you really helped her. Thanks again."

"I think we helped each other Randy."

Jill and I continued our little sex and drugs affair meeting whenever Jill's daughter had a babysitter. It turned out that she loved drugs more than sex. It was okay by me although we shared several hot moments.

Kenny finally talked me into the needle. "I'll help you with the injection. It's a stronger rush like you've never experienced before." He tied up my arm, found a good vein and stuck the needle of ultimate pleasure into me. Instant heaven! Never felt like this ever! I loved life and H.

I became a regular user from that day on. Only mainlining heroin would satisfy my burning desire. I even talked Jill into trying it. I told her to stop by the office when we both knew Randy would be gone for the day.

Three days later Randy was scheduled for an insurance conference downtown. Jill arrived before lunch wearing a short two-piece red outfit. Her legs were amazing. "I don't want a needle mark on my arm," she cautioned.

"Understood. I can inject it behind your knee into the muscle. Same high. You'll love it." She removed her skirt to distract me from the job at hand. We sat on the couch. I injected the H into her. She smiled wildly living in the moment.

That was when Randy wandered into my office. My hand still held the needle. I thought Randy would kill both of us. "YOU BASTARD! WHAT ARE YOU DOING TO MY WIFE?" He punched me in the face. I fell from the couch blood streaming from my nose. Jill didn't move or react at all. She was strung out on her first heroin trip.

When the dust settled, Randy and Jill divorced. I lost my

Jesse's Story

last job I would ever have. I became desperate for money to pay for the heroin. Sold my car, stole money from mom, even pawned the silver candlesticks from my parents' wedding. Heroin had taken over my life. Mom kicked me out with tears running down her face. Nobody would help me. I found out Jill moved back with her parents and wouldn't take my calls. Kenny, my last hope, gave me some heroin for free if I'd just "go away and leave me alone."

starting to have that feeling that need again...how did this happen to me...end up living off a needle...nothing, no one matters anymore...my next dose of H...that magical moment...the craving that will never be satisfied, never goes away...the demon drug that took my soul...

A Story A Day Keeps the EVIL Away

The Great Waldini

The tired face stared out at his old friend. Al dreaded moments like this but the time had come for the talk. The box office needed a boost that The Great Waldini couldn't provide anymore. Perhaps the carnival needed a young stud magician that at least the ladies would respond to even if his act sucked.

"How long we known each other Phil?"

"Gotta be sixteen, seventeen years. We met in Vegas when I was headlining at Caesar's. That's where Margo and I hooked up. She danced at the Riveria and came over every night to see my magic show. Great times Al!"

"Margo," Al's yellow teeth broke into a smile drifting back to those days in Vegas when he signed the rising star to join his traveling carnival. The coffers were overflowing those first five years. "What a babe she was, still has her figure."

Al's face grew serious. "That's not what I wanted to talk about Phil. It's your act. Nobody's in your corner more than me. You ain't drawing flies. Either upgrade your show or else!"

Phil's dark eyes fought back tears. "What am I gonna do? Being a stage magician is all I been doing for twenty-five years.

A Story A Day Keeps the EVIL Away

Even as a kid I'd put on magic shows for the neighbors."

"I can't have a traveling carnival without a magician. When we setup in Tampa, I signed Bruce Grimes, the next David Cooperfield, to headline our opening night. Watch his act and learn from one of the rising illusionists in the magic world."

Phil walked out passing a line of trucks and trailers until he reached his own. "The Great Waldini" read the bright blue letters with a cartoonist drawing of him wearing the purple turban and white gloves. Embarrassing! If they wanted to sell tickets, Margo's hourglass figure in her short stage dress would be much better.

"What'd old Al want this time?" Margo sipped a glass of lemonade as she hemmed her dress, sitting provocatively in her sheer dressing gown.

"The usual. Disappointed with my act. Wants to replace me."

"I told ya. I warned ya this day would come. When Al finally has the balls to fire your ass, I'll be a cocktail waitress again, too old to be a dancer."

Phil's eyes drifted to the fading posters of "The Great Waldini Live at Caesar's" that served as a daily reminder of how far he'd fallen. He remembered all the sold-out shows, the audience of fellow magicians and Vegas entertainers that pushed the tourists into the cheap seats in the back. The magazine interviews, the cover of People, when he and Margo were still in love...

"Why'd you buy these books? Are we made of money?" Margo interrupted his thoughts.

"They're books on magic, even a reprint of "Modern Magic," the first real book of magic from the 1870s."

The Great Waldini

"Didn't know you could read anything but the race results from all the tracks. How much you lose on the horses last month?"

Phil wouldn't take the bait, ignoring her gambling insults. "I want one major trick to add to the act, a showstopper! I've been reading 'bout Harry Houdini. He's the famous escape artist who couldn't be held by handcuffs, prisons, strait jackets, coffins, even a Chinese water torture cell when he hung upside down."

"You're not Houdini, even in your dreams." Margo dropped her gown and switched to a flowery print dress. That always got his attention, a quick flash of her body.

"No it's not the escape part. In 1918," Phil opened one book to the folded page, "Houdini performed at New York's Hippodrome, the largest stage in the world at the time. He made a five ton elephant disappear! That's what I want, a vanishing trick."

"Good," Margo said slipping on her black heels, "'cause I'm gonna vanish right in front of your eyes. I'm going for a walk. I'll leave you to your books."

"David Cooperfield, in one of his TV specials, had a jumbo jet disappear in front of a worldwide audience." At that point Phil knew he was talking to himself. "Don't you remember the Statue of Liberty vanished on live TV?"

The trailer door opened and closed. He was alone. Where did she go on these afternoon walks and who took walks in heels? He suspected that she cheated on him but never pursued it. Maybe today he'd find out the truth.

Before Phil left the trailer, he glanced in the full-length mirror Margo had insisted she needed. Never any fun to see himself. He had more grey hair on his chest than on his head.

A Story A Day Keeps the EVIL Away

The obvious weight gain gave him a gut that he concealed well in baggy stage clothes. But he knew the real story. His rugged good looks had left him years ago, probably why Margo had lost interest in him. Only a business relationship existed between them.

Still, they were married and Phil didn't want to be the source of all the whispers when he walked by their carnival family. He knew where to look first—Samson the Strongman's trailer. Even though Margo had to be seven, eight years older, he watched the two of them exchange glances and smiles right in front of him.

The unlocked door led Phil inside Samson's trailer. Most of the carnival trailers were setup the same, a small kitchen and living area to the right, bedrooms and bath to the left. He didn't have to walk very far. Black heels, the flower print dress, her birthday present last year, lay on the hallway floor followed by her pink undergarments.

Phil had to look for himself. Enough evidence displayed in front of him but he needed to see them together. He took two steps into the bedroom. Margo and Samson rolling around naked in a darkened room became the second worst moment in his life. In first place at age five he walked in on his parents in bed and yelled, "Stop hurting my mom!" He hurried out of the trailer, trying to throw up but couldn't.

What were his options? Fight Samson and get his ass kicked? Divorce Margo and have no partner for his act? Training someone new took time that he didn't have. In a matter of days, he could be out as a magician. Was anyone at the carnival on his side?

The carnival fortune teller, Anastasia, read tarot cards for a living. She came from an East German circus family and left

The Great Waldini

Europe after a tragic fire killed her parents. When Reed, her lion tamer husband, died of a heart attack, she made it clear to Phil of her long-standing feelings for him. He never responded, still she was attractive and available. It had only been six weeks since Reed's sudden death.

Phil looked at her trailer just three down from his. Now was the wrong time. He returned to his trailer and threw the first book he saw against the wall. It crashed and then fell open on the floor. Angry and at the same time curious, Phil lifted the book off the floor. It had opened to a chapter titled, "Black Magic." He didn't recall that being in any of his books. Maybe fate had entered his life. He began reading and reached for paper to jot down some notes. That might work, he thought.

Showtime in forty-five minutes found Margo toweling off after a quick shower. She dressed in her tight, purple sequined dress. Her short blonde wig completed the picture. The mirror reflected back a beautiful woman as she approached forty.

Adjusting the purple turban on his head, Phil wore his matching purple tuxedo coat. With a white shirt, black pants and shoes and then the white gloves he waited to leave for the show tent. Phil stared at Margo as she brushed her hair one last time. Try as he might, he couldn't get the picture of Margo and Samson together out of his head.

The last night of the carnival always pulled in the most customers. Kids came for the rides and cotton candy. Adults pursued the shows and gambling tents, even though the cards were stacked and marked against them. Loud organ music played through the numerous speakers. Several carnival barkers lied in flowery language to encourage people to drop their coins and see the many shows in small colorful tents.

Al entered the magic tent but sat quietly in the back to

A Story A Day Keeps the EVIL Away

watch The Great Waldini. The long, multicolored scarf appeared from Phil's hand and the yellow birds flew from Phil's empty hat. The audience clapped throughout the show. Cutting Margo in half followed by levitating her in the air, what man in the audience didn't fall for Margo's shapely legs? The chemistry Phil and Margo displayed, just like the old days!

Phil ended the show releasing doves into the large crowd. The audience applauded as they rose to leave. Al rushed through the people. "You guys were great! Proud of you two."

"Thanks," Phil acknowledged.

"But I stand by what I said before. You need a new act. Everyone does these tricks."

"I'm working on a new trick, something spectacular. It'll be ready when we open in Tampa."

"I hope so Phil. I'm glad you're taking my threat seriously. The three of us been together for a long time. I want this to continue. Tonight was a step in the right direction." Then he left the tent and joined the crowd outside.

Margo waited until they reached their trailer. "You have a new trick?"

"Not yet," Phil admitted. "Those books you made fun of gave me an idea. A showstopper for all time."

After returning for the second show to a sparse crowd, they packed up their birds, equipment and headed back to the trailer. They separated with Margo taking the main bedroom and with Phil in the spare room that had evolved into his bedroom this past year. At least he didn't have to look at her with the betrayal fresh in his mind.

Sleep wouldn't come for Phil. When eleven turned to midnight then one a.m., Phil got dressed and left the trailer. Who would welcome him at this hour? Only one person he knew.

The Great Waldini

Before he knocked, the trailer door swung open to Anastasia in a red silk robe with her long black hair reaching her waist. "I knew you were coming. The cards told me." Only candlelight illuminated the trailer. Phil started to speak until Anastasia placed two fingers over his mouth. "No words are necessary," she said softly. She kissed him passionately and opened her silk robe revealing – everything. "Follow the candles and share my bed Magic Man."

Teardown Day greeted them at an early hour with the loud noise of the crew taking apart all the tents and loading the trucks for the drive to Tampa. Phil reached for his clothes. Anastasia took his hand instead. "Stay with me forever," she pleaded. "We can leave the carnival and start a new life together."

"I can't," Phil regretted, kissing her willing lips. "There is unfinished business with Margo and the carnival. Maybe after we leave Tampa. I'm sorry but I need to get dressed."

Margo stood over the coffeemaker as he entered the trailer. "Where you been?"

"I'll tell you when you tell me where you really go on your afternoon walks."

She backed down stirring the milk in her coffee. "You feel guilty Phil?"

"I'm taking a shower. We're leaving in less than an hour." He added, "It's a four-and-half hour ride to Tampa."

One of the crew, Stanley Dobbins, drove their trailer. He was a young runaway who liked the constant change of locations. People suspected he left arrest warrants behind in several Northern states. He did his job, stayed sober for the most part and kept out of people's business. Phil's mind wandered to Margo hitting on Stanley next. His cell rang. "Thanks Al. Give him my number."

A Story A Day Keeps the EVIL Away

"Who was that?" Margo asked as she painted her nails.

Before he answered, his cell rang again. "Bruce, the new David Cooperfield, calling me?"

"The Great Waldini. You don't know it yet. I saw your act in Vegas with my parents when I was ten. You were my inspiration man!"

"Thanks. So why are you calling me? We'll be in Tampa by noon. We can talk face-to-face in a few hours."

"Got this idea Phil. I would be honored to have you on stage with me. Maybe give you ten minutes. What'd say Phil?"

"That would be great. I have a new disappearing trick I wanted to try. Look forward to meeting you and working out the details."

"Bye Phil."

Black Magic dominated Phil's thoughts. A chance existed to impress a standing-room-only audience and reestablish his reputation as an illusionist. And have Margo pay for her betrayal. Back to the mysterious chapter he stumbled upon and create the showstopper people would talk about for years and years.

What bitch took Phil in last night and how many other times did it happen, Margo wondered. Samson occupied her thoughts and desires. But Phil married her and if they broke up, she would be out of the carnival. She needed to keep an eye on him.

Signs for Tampa brought an end to their trip. Less than an hour to go, Phil left the living area taking his book to the bathroom. He spoke the ancient words and stretched his hands over the sink. Real flames appeared from his fingers! Damn, he thought, the old magic worked. In the early days magicians were connected with witches and the occult. How else could real magic happen unless the devil himself whispered into the

The Great Waldini

magician's ear? Today, Phil could use Black Magic and be admired again as a genius.

Before setting up for tonight's opening performance, Al provided tables of salads, chicken and desserts for everyone to enjoy. Phil and Margo sat together. Her eyes followed his as he exchanged smiles with Anastasia. The widow, of course, Margo should have guessed.

Bruce Grimes arrived shaking hands, signing autographs and taking pictures with the carnival family. Then he walked over to Phil. "The Great Waldini, we meet at last." Handing his camera to Margo, he added,"Please take our picture. Thanks."

"Let's walk and talk Bruce," Phil suggested rising from the table.

"My show van is here. My guys are ready to unload when the tent's up." They walked away.

Margo stared at Anastasia thinking, I never liked that dark-haired bitch. I want revenge on both of them. Something that would send a scare to Anastasia and an embarrassment to Phil in front of that huge opening night audience.

Late afternoon the large main tent filled with rows of wooden chairs and an array of colored lights. Bruce Grimes directed his men as the massive equipment covered the stage. "Very impressive," Phil said joining Bruce in the middle of the stage. "I'm not used to the big stage anymore. They have me working the small tent. The animal acts usually open here."

"Not tonight my friend." Bruce patted him on the back. "It's a magical night. Here's my plan. I'll open and say forty to forty-five minutes in I'll introduce you and leave the stage. Say ten minutes later, I'll return and go another hour."

"You never met Margo, my wife and stage assistant. She will disappear in front of everyone. No mirrors, real magic

A Story A Day Keeps the EVIL Away

Bruce." Phil climbed down the steps. "See you before the show starts."

Phil pulled the folded paper from his shirt pocket. The strange words of another time yet the perfect words for the perfect trick. Margo will vanish from the world tonight, never to return! Unlike the past mirrored cabinet that masked her disappearance, this Black Magic he could direct but never control. Top that Bruce Grimes!

He passed Anastasia's trailer and fought the urge to enjoy the afternoon with her. More practicing and checking the cabinet for tonight represented the keys for success. For his dream to be with Anastasia soon, this night would guarantee their future together. Bye bye Margo!

The afternoon turned to early evening. Cars and trucks parked everywhere and people stood in long lines. Excitement and organ music filled the air. Al couldn't help but smile over the successful booking of the next David Cooperfield.

Margo rushed into the trailer, nearly out of breath. "Sorry, I had something I had to do. I'll be ready on time Phil."

Phil adjusted his purple turban in the mirror. Did Margo have the nerve to visit Samson and almost miss their biggest show in years? Concentrate, concentrate on the words, the hand movements.

Twenty minutes later they waited in the back of the stage for their moment. "It's the same cabinet we've used before Phil. How's this vanishing trick any different?"

"You'll see Margo, you'll see. Just stay inside the cabinet. That's essential for the trick to work."

Bruce Grimes announced, "I would like to introduce the man who I consider my mentor and new friend, The Great Waldini!"

The Great Waldini

They both appeared waving to thunderous applause, like the old Vegas days. "Thanks for the kind words Bruce. I'm also a big fan of yours!" Bruce bowed slightly and left the stage.

The crew rolled the cabinet on the stage as Phil said, "My assistant and my wife Margo!" He waited for the clapping to stop. "Margo will disappear before your eyes tonight!" Phil opened the cabinet so the audience could view the inside. Then he continued, "Say goodbye to Margo." Margo stepped inside the cabinet and Phil spun it around twice.

Margo had already slipped through the false bottom and under the stage. Now was the hard part, taking Anastasia all tied up and gagged and pushing her through the false bottom and into the cabinet.

The Great Waldini uttered the ancient sounds. Flames appeared from his fingertips. The stage lights blinked nearly turning off. A cold wind entered the tent. The trance like feeling overpowered him as his arms flew violently in the air. Then he stopped. Margo was gone forever!

Phil threw open the cabinet doors, nothing, no one inside. It really worked. The crowd erupted in loud applause. Suddenly Margo appeared in the audience walking up the stage steps. Bruce returned to the stage. "Great trick Phil. You fooled everyone." He extended a hand to Margo and helped her back on stage.

"That's not the trick. Something went wrong." A pale Phil stared at Margo. "Why are you here?"

A confused Margo explained, "I don't know what you did but Anastasia was in the cabinet. I put her there myself. You made her disappear!"

A Story A Day Keeps the EVIL Away

Don't Speak Ill of the Dead

The full moon reflected on the dark still waters of Lake Tecumseh. Only the occasional movement of the oars disturbed the silent night. The beam of a flashlight guided the small row boat to the middle of the lake.

"That's good Jake. We'll stop here." Marvin stood up awkwardly trying to balance his tall, overweight body. "That son bitch don't deserve a proper burial."

"Let's get this over with." Jake looked down at the large dead body on the bottom of the boat. Damn knife had nearly decapitated him.

"You tie those cement buckets to his legs like I told ya?"

"Yea Marv. I'm scared being out here." His small frame shivered in the cool night air.

"Shut up! Come on and help me throw Ricky Sikes to his watery grave. I hate that bastard!"

"Don't say that. You'll be cursed if you speak that way about the dead. It's a Shawnee curse!"

"Sikes' only part injun."

"Not talkin 'bout him. It's Lake Tecumseh, named after a

A Story A Day Keeps the EVIL Away

Shawnee Indian chief." Jake explained.

"You're weak. I ought to throw you down there too. Grab his other leg. One, two, three, over the side."

A large splash from the body hitting the water drenched Jake in cold lake water. "Damnit Marv I'm all wet!"

"Shut up and starting rowing." Marvin's flashlight beam tried in vain to watch Ricky Sikes' final descent to the bottom of the lake. But the cement buckets did their job and the body disappeared from sight.

"Why don't you do some rowing too?" Jake asked.

"I'm paying you, ain't I?" Marvin turned the flashlight beam into Jake's face. "And don't even think 'bout going to the cops. Plenty a room in the lake for another body. You can sleep with that damn lowlife for all eternity."

"I'd never rat on you Marv. How long we know each other? Probably junior high." Jake feared Marvin but wanted his friendship and protection. "Lemme tell ya 'bout Tecumseh." Jake changed the subject.

"What's this Shawnee curse?"

"Tecumseh's Shawnee tribe was hunted by General William Henry Harrison. Same guy that became president."

"So?"

"Tecumseh cursed all the Great Chiefs as he called the presidents. Said every president elected in zero ending years would die in office. Harrison died and so did Lincoln, Garfield, McKinley and Kennedy. You don't wanna mess with the spirit world Marv."

"That's a bunch of crap! Not afraid of dead Indians!" A coyote glared at them from the dock before running away. They reached the shore. Between the two men the row boat was flipped onto the Ford's truck bed.

Don't Speak Ill of the Dead

"You can stay at my place till morning. Have a few beers to celebrate Ricky's death," Marvin said to Jake. Marvin drove through the empty streets until they completed the forty minute drive to the cabin. "Help me put that boat out back."

After they moved the boat, Marvin pulled out the hose and let the powerful rush of water clean out the row boat. They went inside the cabin. Jake hurried to the bathroom. The hot water and soap worked their magic on his blood covered hands. Jake watched his hands shake from the night's deadly events. Better not tell Marv he thought.

Marvin tossed Jake a can of Budweiser beer as he finished his second can. "I'm glad he's dead. Always being a smart ass, always insulting me in front of my girl." He spit on the floor. "That's all I got for you Ricky." He reached for his next beer.

Jake sat down on the worn plaid couch. He covered his right hand with his left to stop the shaking. Then he quickly downed his beer. "Marv, think I'll go lay down. I'm not feeling too good."

"You never were much of a drinker. Yea, go ahead and sleep. I"ll pay ya in the morning." Marvin crushed the can in his right hand reaching for another beer with his left. Sometime between beers eight and nine, Marvin passed out on the couch spilling most of the last beer on the couch and floor. He snored heavily. Suddenly the air filled with thick black smoke. Damn cabin's on fire, he realized stumbling towards the door.

Marvin crashed onto the ground hearing Jake's screams from inside the burning cabin. The large yellow-orange flames enveloped the cabin's only door. Sorry Jake, he fought to wake up, you were kind of a loser anyhow. Not much of a loss. Scrambling to his Ford truck, Marvin gripped his keys tightly. Time to get the hell outta Dodge. Let the fire department deal with this mess. Jake, nice knowing ya, not really. But the bigger question

A Story A Day Keeps the EVIL Away

Marvin tried to understand was who wanted him dead?

Could Ricky Sikes come back from the bottom of that damn Indian lake and kill him? Maybe Jake was right 'bout something—the power of the Shawnee curse! The hell with both of those assholes! Jake probably dropped a lit cigarette or joint and burned down the cabin. Marvin gunned the engine and drove through town to his house. He fumbled for the right key. Finally he staggered down the small hallway falling on top of his bed.

Loud, repeated banging on his front door pulled Marvin out of his drunken dream of Ricky Sikes rising from Lake Tecumseh and dragging him under the water to his death. What idiot would bother him on a Sunday morning? "WHAT!" He yelled opening the door. Then he saw Grace, his Grace, standing in front of him. Even a simple white t-shirt and jeans never looked so good. She had big blonde hair like an old rock video. And that ass! Amazing Grace.

"Marvin your breath smells like a sewer. I kept calling you last night and you never picked up. Didn't you get my texts?"

"Sorry doll. Guess I drank too much. Come on in. Why you here so early? I wanted to sleep till noon."

She walked in and sat in the nearest chair. "Gotta call that your cabin burned down. I thought you were dead."

"It'll take more than that to kill me." He leaned towards her for a kiss.

"MARVIN! You rinse out your mouth before you kiss me!"

Marvin responded, "Lemme get some sleep. I'll buy you dinner later, your choice of restaurants, except that Chinese place."

Grace kissed his cheek. "Call me," she said heading for her car.

Don't Speak Ill of the Dead

But sleep didn't come for Marvin. Tossing and turning for over an hour, he gave up and took a shower. Just as he buttoned his shirt, another knock on the door. No one was there. How strange, he thought. A coyote ran into the open field by his house.

Sammy's Grill and Lounge had the best steaks and the best variety of beers. Anyone trying to drink a beer from each country represented was usually carried out and dumped in the parking lot. As they approached the doors, Grace dazzled in a long red dress with a slit on both sides and matching red heels. Marvin wore all black clothes with black boots. Blaring country music greeted them when they entered Sammy's.

"Only two of us," Marvin repeated to the hostess. They found a corner table in the back. Still elevated voices were needed to communicate through the loud music. "Jake died in the cabin fire." Marvin told her after placing their orders.

"How do you know that?" Grace acted surprised.

"He's staying at the cabin for a few days. A little trouble with his wife. He wasn't the brightest person you'll ever meet. Probably started the fire doing something stupid."

"That's not very nice. I thought he was your friend."

"Yea, a dead friend." Marvin took a long drink of his beer.

She frowned. "The Shawnee tribe lived in this area for many years. There's probably Indian spirits around us. Be careful what you say!"

"Not that again!" He gulped down his beer and held the empty mug over his head hoping the waitress would notice.

"I don't like you when you act this way!" They sat quietly waiting for their food. Marvin began checking out the young waitresses walking by, ignoring Grace's icy stare. Their waitress, Becka, an attractive brunette in a cowboy hat, delivered

A Story A Day Keeps the EVIL Away

a tray of food. Grace looked at her sirloin steak dinner while Marvin's eyes followed Becka until she walked out of sight.

When Becka returned, she smiled at Marvin. Her dark brown eyes locked into his blue eyes. "How about some dessert tonight?"

"What I want's not on the menu." Marvin laughed loudly.

"NOTHING FOR US!" Grace responded in a steely tone.

"We'll have the check Becka thanks." Grace watched him watch her walk away.

"Give me your keys! I'll wait in the truck!" She grabbed the keys from his outstretched hand.

Becka approached the table again. Marvin, without Grace's disapproval to deal with, waved a twenty dollar bill. "That's your tip if I get your number."

"Sure your girlfriend won't mind." She gave her sexiest smile. A twenty dollar tip would be nice.

Handing over his cell phone, he said, "Put your number in Becka. Don't worry about my date." He dropped a fifty on the table for the bill and touched her hand as he retrieved his cell from her.

Marvin swung the restaurant doors open as he headed for Grace and his truck. There would be no goodnight kiss or any other fun tonight. At least he got a number from that hot waitress.

Exploding in front of him, his truck roared with flames. The power of the blast knocked him backwards onto the sidewalk. He jumped to his feet and ran to the fiery truck. Several other people in the parking lot rushed over trying to stop him. "Grace, Grace, oh no! Not you!" He felt real tears for the first time in his life. Grace couldn't be saved. He dropped to his knees and cried into his hands.

Don't Speak Ill of the Dead

Was it bad luck or revenge? He didn't know or care. I should be in that truck, he thought, I should be dead. Not Grace. Not Grace. Police Officer Morse drove him back to his house. "Are you gonna be alright sir? Is there someone I can call for you?"

"No. No, there's no one. Thanks for the ride." Marvin entered the house and sat in the dark for hours. Finally an idea, the only possible idea, formed in his mind. Time to return to Lake Tecumseh and confront dead Ricky Sikes.

With his truck gone forever, Marvin opened the garage hoping his Harley would start up. It did and he rode through the darkness trying to avoid the rain drops of an approaching storm. He left his motorcycle in the small parking lot and walked straight to the lake. The rain increased in intensity but it didn't matter, nothing mattered.

"RICKY! Damn you Ricky! You come face me you son bitch!" He screamed into the storm. Marvin took his first steps into Lake Tecumseh. "Ricky, where are you?" He continued heading into the cold water. Knee high, waist high, and nearly chest high. "RICKY! Face me you coward! You took my Grace from me!"

Then the water reached his shoulders as he moved deeper and deeper into the lake. "RICKY!" The final word spoken by Marvin. A coyote trotted back into the woods.

"It's the damnedest thing," Officer Morse said to the other police officers. "When the divers pulled Marvin's body outta the lake, he had two cement cans wrapped around his neck. Craziest suicide you'll ever see. Never would've found him if it hadn't been that 911 call from a guy claiming to be Ricky Sikes."

A Story A Day Keeps the EVIL Away

The Hanging Judge

The stagecoach bounced along the uneven ground. Jarred awake, Jeremiah Potter escaped from that strange dream. A woman dressed all in white from head to toe, including a white veil covering her entire face, ran towards him. What did it mean? His mother had died years ago in Kansas. Not her. And his one and only lady love, Sarah, caught the fever back East never joining him for the planned wedding and their life together. A family funeral replaced the wedding.

"Excuse me." A pleasant female voice called out.

Potter looked up at the beautiful blonde haired passenger sitting across from him. She wore a red dress trimmed in lace. Her soft blue eyes pulled him in. "Yes? Sorry I drifted off." Potter explained still waking up.

"We were never introduced." She reached out her right hand. "Maggie Bridges. I'm the new owner of the Gold Rush Saloon in Dawson City."

"Glad to meet you Maggie. Name's Jeremiah Potter. I've gotta job waiting for me too." He shook her small hand, noticing all the gold rings.

A Story A Day Keeps the EVIL Away

"If you don't mind, I'm surprised to see a man in a tailored suit." Does he have money, she wondered.

Outside the stagecoach, yelling, shooting, the stagecoach stopped suddenly. Maggie fell forward nearly in Potter's lap. She pulled back blushing and then reached down the front of her dress. Her hand retrieved the tiny derringer. "My little protection," she said to Potter.

"Harlan, you get the strong box. I'll get the passengers." A gruff voice commanded, "You get on out here. Nobody gets hurt."

Potter jumped out and reached back for Maggie's hand. Maggie came out gripping her derringer.

"Wow Judge Potter! I'm right sorry to bother you sir." His harsh voice changed quickly to a scared little boy's. "You and that pretty lady please get back on the stagecoach." Then he yelled, "Harlan, you put that strong box back. We're riding out."

They rode off in a cloud of dust. Harlan spoke first, "Why'd you change your mind Luke? That strong box was heavy."

Luke answered, "Judge Potter, the hanging judge, was riding inside. Don't need that kinda trouble."

In the stagecoach Maggie laughed. "Judge Potter! You seem young to be a judge. But I heard of you, everyone has." She tried to calm down. All this excitement and a chance to shoot a man for the first time combined to make her head spin.

Potter always thought his neatly trimmed brown hair and handlebar mustache made him appear older. It didn't. He smiled back. "Growing up in Kansas, I could have been the worst cowboy ever. Tried roping, all I caught was myself. Fell off horses. Couldn't shoot straight. But I was good with books so I went to school and became a judge."

The Hanging Judge

Maggie chuckled at his stories. "Nice to know someone with legal power. Might need your help someday." She returned his smile. "Look neither one of us has friends waiting in Dawson City. Maybe we can have dinner together? Girl's gotta eat."

"I accept your invitation Maggie Bridges. Actually I do know Sheriff John Ward. We've conducted business before. Gotta prisoner set for trial tomorrow. I'm the presiding judge for the Dakota territory."

The remaining hours passed quickly until the stagecoach arrived in Dawson City. Did Potter's eyes ever turn from Maggie? He noticed the stagecoach slowing then stopping. "Dawson City already?"

A large man dressed in black from his black hat to his dust-covered black boots stood on the street. He approached the stagecoach helping Maggie to the ground. "Nice to meet you miss." His dark eyes followed her but he greeted Potter. "Jeremiah, how was your trip?"

"Sheriff, how can I complain? You saw my traveling companion." He felt small compared to the six foot four broad chested sheriff. Ward looked like the West, a tough, hard man with the gunfighter's shoot first approach. His Colt revolver rested in his black holster. No wonder there weren't a whole lot of trials in Dawson City. Outlaws got buried, not tried.

"Set you up in the Manor Hotel like last time. We can pay for two nights and your meals. That okay judge?" Ward continued talking, "Stop by after you've settle in. We could have some dinner."

Potter snatched up his heavy bag. "I will check in with you later. But I got plans for dinner."

Maggie Bridges led the stagecoach driver down the street juggling her three large suitcases. A lady never carried her own

A Story A Day Keeps the EVIL Away

bags. The swinging doors to the Gold Rush Saloon were held open for her. A lady never opened doors either. She caught herself laughing when the doors slammed against the stagecoach driver spilling her bloomers, corsets, and hoop skirts.

"Maggie?" A short but wide bodied man asked. A large graying beard decorated his face while a silk sleeve garter decorated his white shirt. "I'm Johnson the bartender, bookkeeper, whatever you need." They shook hands, hers disappeared inside the vise grip of his. "I'll take your suitcases."

She turned, kissed the stagecoach driver on the cheek and handed him two silver dollars. "Thanks Bart. You gotta free drink any time in my place." Maggie followed Johnson upstairs to a bedroom in the far corner. "Thanks Mr. Johnson. I'll be down shortly."

Jeremiah Potter rested then bathed before dressing for dinner. He reached the front desk and found a note waiting for him. "Jeremiah, dinner at my saloon around seven. Maggie." His gold pocket watch showed nearly seven so he headed for the Gold Rush Saloon.

Maggie was a vision in a midnight blue dress enlarged by a hoop underskirt and trimmed in white. Her blonde hair flowed past her shoulders. Extra rouge and blue eye shadow gave her face a stunning appearance. She waited in a quiet backroom away from the bar patrons and noise. Johnson led Potter through the bar to the small room.

"Judge, good evening," she greeted him.

"Please call me Jeremiah," he said kissing her outstretched hand.

"Not sure what you like to drink with dinner so I thought we'd start with a pot of hot coffee."

Potter poured the coffee into the small cups handing

The Hanging Judge

Maggie hers. "Did Johnson tell you we have to use your saloon for our courtroom tomorrow? No other place large enough in town."

"Oh, that's okay." She sipped her coffee. "I've heard that hanging is good for business. I'm sure we'll be busy after the trial ends."

Johnson returned carrying two plates of steaks and potatoes. They ate quietly although their eyes kept meeting. Maggie reached across the table lightly touching his hand. "Wait till you see dessert. It's upstairs." She laughed sensuously.

As Potter followed her up the stairs, he noticed, "There's a lot of buttons on the back of your dress."

"We have all night," she teased. He chased her up the final steps.

The Gold Rush Saloon was completely rearranged for the morning trial. Three long tables were set up in front of the bar. Johnson and Granger, the night bartender, finished moving chairs by the tables. "Remember," Johnson advised to the young Granger, "no drinks can be served till the trial's over."

Judge Potter walked in hoping for hot coffee before the proceedings commenced. That dream of the woman dressed in white had visited him again. He settled his bag on the middle table and removed his gavel and the Blackstone Law book placing them next to the bag. Johnson surprised Potter with a cup of coffee. "Much appreciated," he said in Johnson's direction. Potter wore his black suit, white shirt and black string tie. All business today with a man's life at stake.

The faint smell of lilacs reached him before he saw Maggie. "Morning judge," she whispered in his direction. He tried not to react. But last night's activities brought a smile to his face. He watched her yellow dress until she sat down in the back.

A Story A Day Keeps the EVIL Away

Then the townspeople were allowed in the saloon. The tables filled quickly with several people standing by the doors. The talking started. "That's the hanging judge!" "Going to see a real show today." "Is that Potter up front?" "Where's Sheriff Ward?" "I'm taking my boy to his first hanging."

The noise level increased when Sheriff John Ward brought his handcuffed prisoner, Billy Burke, through the crowd. Burke was an unshaven man with wild hair, a burly man in his thirties. He had no friends in this room. The crowd parted out of the way not wanting to incur Ward's wrath or to receive a sharp elbow in the gut. Ward pushed his prisoner into the chair next to him at the side table.

Mr. Frank Moore sat at the opposite table. He owned the Dawson Livery Stables and served as the prosecuting attorney. Even in his best suit, his dark bearded face gave him the appearance of a lumberjack, not a lawyer.

A nervous, thin man named Ben Adair hurried to join Ward and Burke. He represented the defense and he met the prisoner for the first time fifteen minutes ago in his cell. Adair knew everybody hated the defense attorney.

Potter banged his gavel loudly until the room quieted. "I bring this court to order. I'm U.S. District Judge Jeremiah Potter presiding judge for the Dakota territory. I see Mr. Moore is our prosecutor and, let me find the name I was handed, Mr. Adair for the defense. Proceed Mr. Moore with your opening remarks."

"Your honor, people of Dawson City, what we have here today is a ruthless murderer who needs to pay for his crimes." Moore sat down.

Adair stood fumbling and nearly dropping his notes. "My client is an honest man falsely accused your honor."

The Hanging Judge

Potter said, "Mr. Moore continue." He tried hard to listen to every word although he couldn't help noticing Maggie's yellow dress complementing her blonde hair.

"I call my first witness, Duke Connors." A gangling man in his late twenties, Duke sat down in the front chair. "Swear him in Bud." Moore waited and then began, "The night of August twelfth, you were walking past my livery stable. What did you see Duke?"

"Yes sir. I was drunk but I seen that horse thief over there." Duke heard the crowd's laughter and waved.

"Mr. Connors," Judge Potter commanded, "this is a court of law!"

"Sorry your honor. I was saying that cowboy drew on old Hank Reynolds. Shot him right in the head."

"Thank you. Your turn Mr. Adair." Moore walked back to his table.

Adair stood, "No questions your honor." Then he sat down.

Billy Burke growled, "You trying to get me hung!"

Sheriff Ward's left elbow connected with Burke's face and the prisoner was silent.

"For my next witness I call Sheriff John Ward. Swear in the sheriff Bud." Moore reviewed his notes and looked up at the sheriff. "Sheriff Ward, you led the posse that caught Billy Burke."

"That's right. Not much of a chase. We tracked him down the same night. Told me he shot old Hank and stole his horse."

"That's a damn lie!" Burke jumped to his feet.

"SHUT UP AND SIT DOWN!" Potter yelled.

"Anything else sheriff?" Moore asked.

"The horse belonged to Hank."

Adair approached Sheriff Ward. "Do you hate Mr. Burke?"

77

A Story A Day Keeps the EVIL Away

"I hate his guts! Should've shot him!" The crowd roared.

"That's all your honor." Adair returned to his chair. Ward grabbed the other chair next to Burke.

"Judge, I'm finished." Moore turned to Adair. "All yours son."

Adair announced, "I call Mrs. Burke to the stand." An older woman emerged from the crowd and sat in the front chair. "What is your relation to Mr. Burke?"

"He's my son. He's not a bad boy just can't stay out of trouble since his pa died." She dabbed a handkerchief to her wet eyes. "Please don't kill my Billy," she pleaded with Judge Potter.

"No questions your honor," Moore said from his chair.

Mrs. Burke walked back stopping in front of Billy; then she returned to the back of the saloon.

Adair spoke, "We're done."

"Mr. Moore?" Potter turned to the prosecutor.

"Billy Burke is a cold blooded killer and a horse thief. He murdered Hank Reynolds. He needs to hang judge."

Adair asserted, "All Mr. Moore proved is my client is a horse thief. The only witness to the shooting was a drunk cowboy. Let Mr. Burke go to prison. Don't hang him your honor."

Judge Potter sat quietly for a moment. He'd hung men for less evidence than this. He spoke loudly for the whole room to hear, "Mr. Adair stand with your client." He waited briefly and continued, "As presiding judge of the Dakota territory I find you guilty of murder. Billy Burke you shall hang by the neck until dead. May god have mercy on your soul." Potter hammered down his gavel one final time.

There was a scramble through the swinging doors as people hurried to witness the hanging of Billy Burke. Sheriff Ward slammed the struggling prisoner against the table. Then he

The Hanging Judge

shoved him forward to the waiting rope. The gallows were built opposite the town's hardware store. Ward and Burke climbed the steps while people cheered.

Judge Potter grabbed his bag from the table turning towards the bar. "Not watching the hanging judge?" Johnson asked.

"No. Once you've seen somebody's neck stretched till death, they're all the same. Only the time it takes differs." Potter sat at the bar. "How 'bout some eggs Mr. Johnson?"

"Sure, but you better move over to one of the corner tables. That crowd's coming directly here to drink when the hanging's over." Spying Granger, he yelled out, "Hey Granger get them tables outta the way!"

Maggie Bridges was waiting for him. "Jeremiah, thought I'd sit with you before all the chaos starts. I'll be serving drinks for the rest of the day."

"Too bad. Maybe later?" Potter said hopefully.

"We'll see." A loud roar came from the streets. "They're on the way. Gotta bring the girls downstairs. I found out Annie plays the piano. Gotta go. Sorry."

With the Gold Rush the only saloon in Dawson City, the entire town pushed and shoved their way through the doors. Yelling drink orders, the screaming happy crowd couldn't wait to share their views on the hanging of Billy Burke. Poker games broke out. Annie's piano playing was drown out by the uproar.

As Potter finished his eggs, two townspeople approached him. "This is for you judge." Two large whiskey glasses were quickly joined by four more from the delighted crowd. Heavy slams on his back nearly caused him to choke on his first drink. No one realized a simple "thanks" was enough.

Potter knew he couldn't drink very much without passing

A Story A Day Keeps the EVIL Away

out. Even with pretty girls gathered around his table, the third drink sent his head spinning. People appeared to double and triple everywhere. His head hit the table.

Potter's eyes tried to focus on Mr. Johnson who practically carried him from the Gold Rush to the Manor Hotel. He mumbled some words in Johnson's direction but he was already gone. No use in fighting the urge to sleep. Potter passed out.

The woman in white reached out to him again in his dreams.

Loud banging on his room door accompanied shouting, "POTTER, JUDGE POTTER! OPEN THE DOOR!"

Jeremiah Potter stared through the darkness and swung his legs to the floor. "I'm coming. Hold on." When he opened the door, he wondered how he ended up dressed in his red long johns.

In a normal situation, Sheriff Ward would have laughed at his attire. This was not normal in any way. "I need you to get dressed in a hurry and come with me."

"What's happening sheriff?"

"Got your girl Maggie locked up behind bars. She killed Duke Connors. Shot him between the eyes with her little gun."

Potter changed into his clothes and followed Ward out of the hotel. "Town's angry. Duke was real popular though he's got the brains of a mule. Nobody knows Maggie. She's just a saloon girl to them." Ward explained.

Sheriff Ward pushed through the crowd that had gathered outside his office. People's voices were mad. "Gotta hang her!" 'I can't believe old Duke is dead." "Me and Duke grew up together. She's gotta pay!" "Look it's the hanging judge. We'll have justice now." "Somebody get a rope."

"You keep that shotgun handy," Ward said to Deputy Clay

The Hanging Judge

Hardin as he closed the door. Clay had been the town sheriff until his hair turned silver and his gun hand slowed. But Ward knew he could count on Clay if it all went to hell around him.

Potter rushed to Maggie sitting on a bench crying into her hands. He reached his handkerchief through the bars. "Here Maggie. Tell me what happened."

She wiped away the tears saying, "Those cowboys been grabbing at me all night. I know they're drunk. I've worked in bars for awhile now. But this guy throws me against the wall kissing me pawing on me. I just lost it. I pushed my derringer against his forehead and pulled the trigger. There's blood all over my dress." Her eyes filled with tears.

"Can you handle a gun?" Ward came up behind Potter.

"No. I'd probably shoot myself."

"That crowd's growing and they're liquored up. I don't wanna shoot these people. I could name everybody outside after all these years in Dawson City. But I will shoot if I have to."

Maggie sobbed, "I don't wanna die sheriff."

Ward looked at Potter. "You can walk through those people peacefully. We gotta back door we never use. If you could get a couple horses, have Johnson help you. I'll deal with the town. Hurry!"

Judge Potter tried to slip through the crowd but was greeted as the town's hero. Handshakes, pats on the back, he headed to the Gold Rush Saloon. Poker games continued as did drinking throughout the bar. Duke's body had been carried out through the kitchen. Some people never realized what happened.

"Johnson, I need your help." Potter explained the escape plan.

"I've got a buggy I could load up Maggie's suitcases. Get your stuff together and meet me in the alley." Johnson

A Story A Day Keeps the EVIL Away

responded.

"Thanks. And Maggie needs a clean dress to wear."

Moments later, Potter ran down the alley tossing his heavy bag onto the buggy. Johnson said, "You have fresh horses, got most of today's money from the bar for you too." He shook Potter's hand. "Good luck to you. All my best to Maggie."

Potter lightly knocked on the rear door holding the dress, a white dress, that Johnson had selected. Ward opened the door.

Potter handed Maggie the white dress in her open cell. Ward shoved a piece of paper into Potter's hand. "That's my brother's name. He's a riverboat captain. I'll telegraph him tomorrow and tell him you'll be there by the end of the week." Ward couldn't help looking as Maggie slipped off and on the dresses. "I'll create a big commotion out front. You two ride fast and don't look back. Duke was a jackass, not worth dying for. You keep that pretty lady safe."

"Thanks for everything. I owe you sheriff," Potter said.

"Might collect on that someday. Cover her face just in case." Ward waited till they walked out the back door. Then he opened the front door. He shot his pistol into the air. "Now you folks go home. Sleep it off. Only thing waiting in there for you is Clay's shotgun." He slammed the door shut.

Maggie reached into her suitcase retrieving a white veil to cover her face. The woman in white, the woman of his dreams, Jeremiah Potter smiled at his luck and led the buggy out of Dawson City.

Deadly Desire

I woke up face down on a dirt covered road. My entire body ached and bled. I tried to raise my left arm but it only moved inches. Something burned on my forearm like I was branded with a hot iron. No street lights, no lights of any kind. I'm surrounded by the night. Can't even move my body off the road. Maybe the pain will go away if I die here in the dark.

Bright lights, headlights, moved quickly towards my mangled body. This is how it ends run over by a car in the middle of nowhere. The lights stopped in front of me. Suddenly a female in white illuminated by the headlights (an angel?) walked towards me. "Oh my god!" I heard her say then I passed out again.

I remember being lifted onto a stretcher and the loud, blaring sound of the ambulance. Incoherent voices talked to me. Nothing made sense. Everything was blurry. I fought hard to stay awake. People kept talking around me. "He's lucky to be alive...lost a lot of blood." "I've done all I can for him." "The police want to talk to him when he regains consciousness."

My mind saw Isabella's cover girl face, the source of my

A Story A Day Keeps the EVIL Away

greatest joy and my greatest pain. Her long black hair cascaded over the white pillow case. A pear shaped diamond necklace drew my eyes to her sensuous ebony body. Laughing, happy, she enjoyed the moment with me. Isabella's soft brown eyes invited me to a world of pleasure.

Isabella screamed! Then the pain began.

I recall being thrown from the bed against the far wall. Gilley stood over me. His menacing six foot frame had a muscular build from his obsession with the weight room. "YOU BASTARD!" He kicked me in the stomach. I gasped for breath. "And robbing me too!" He emptied the briefcase covering me in a sea of fifty and hundred dollar bills.

Isabella ran from the bedroom wrapped in a sheet crying loudly. Taz, Gilley's henchman a mountain of muscles and tattoos, rushed in. "What happened?"

"Mac was in bed with my wife!"

Taz jammed a silver revolver against my head. "Just say the word Gilley."

"Not here. Drag his ass behind the house in the woods." Then Gilley looked at me. "I won't kill you. But when we're done with you you'll be begging for a bullet to your head!"

"She loves me Gilley." I blurted out.

Taz's boot smashed into my face. The next few hours I was in and out of consciousness. The beating brought me to a new level of pain throughout my body. I heard Gilley say something about calling Joshua, Gilley's tattoo guy, "to come over right now. You and Joshua dump his body couple hours from town."

I woke up on the dirt road and again in a hospital bed. A warm hand in mine. A woman's voice. "I'm alone in the world since my divorce is final. No reason to hurry home just Checkers my cat waiting for me. I hope you wake soon. There's

Deadly Desire

so much I want to share with you."

My eyes tried to focus. A nurse sat next to my hospital bed. I attempted to smile at her instead I moaned. The cute nurse had blondish brown hair, dark, expressive eyes and reacted with a big smile when I opened my eyes.

"Hi. Welcome back." She greeted me.

"Were you the one who found me, who saved me that night?"

"Yes I did. I take that shortcut to the hospital when I'm running late and I'm always running late. There's no traffic. It saves me ten minutes every day." She paused and gripped my hand tighter. "I almost didn't see you. I could have run you over." A tear ran down her cheek.

"But you didn't. I'm alive thanks to you." I returned her smile even though my face hurt. "How long have I been here?"

"One week tomorrow. You were in a coma for days. I didn't know if you would come back to me. I sit with you every day on my breaks and after my shift's over. You have blue eyes. I haven't seen them till now."

"I'm sure you have lots of questions for me."

"You've mumbled some names in your sleep like Gilley, Taz, and Isabella many times. I hope you're not married."

"I'm not. No kids either. Let me rest. We'll talk tomorrow. And thanks again for saving my life." I passed out and didn't hear her leave.

The next day I spent with doctors and medical tests. Everyone seemed happy that I had returned from the dead. Nobody asked me my opinion to be back among the living. Maybe it would have been better for everyone to have died on that dirt road.

Still, I longed for my dark beauty Isabella, my reason to

A Story A Day Keeps the EVIL Away

keep living. Would I ever see her again? The welcome mat will definitely not be out for me if I go back.

My dinner tray arrived. Hunger dominated my thoughts until I saw a bowl of soup, crackers and orange jello. I used the straws for my drinks. Based on my sore jaw I couldn't chew anything hard. I had my last spoon of jello when she walked in my room. "There you are," I said. My nurse friend had arrived. She removed my tray and sat next to me.

"We haven't been introduced. I'm Kate Mathews. No one knows your name. You're listed as John Doe." Her hand slipped into mine.

"Everyone calls me Mac."

"Are you able to answer my questions? The police detective said you couldn't remember what happened."

"For you I'll answer anything."

"Who beat you up and nearly killed you?"

"That would be Gilley."

"Who's Gilley?"

"My brother. A dangerous man. He's involved in drugs and guns. Not the man to cross."

"Who's Isabella?"

"The reason I'm in the hospital. Gilley's wife. We were gonna run off together with a briefcase full of Gilley's drug money."

Kate dropped my hand. "Maybe I have judged you all wrong."

"I'm not a bad guy. Just got crazy over the wrong woman. The other name you mentioned Taz is a big mean dude. Avoid him at all costs."

Kate stood and looked at me. "You'll be able to leave the hospital in a few days. I thought about offering my home to you. I'm not sure. Can you explain your tattoo?"

Deadly Desire

"What tattoo?" She pulled off the long bandage on my left forearm revealing, DONT COME BACK. "I didn't ask for that." I explained.

"You need my help. I'll take you home on a trial basis. We'll see how it goes." She left the room.

The day finally came and I rolled along in the wheelchair to Kate's waiting car. My legs were gaining their strength from my daily walks down the hospital hallways. My left arm remained weak though.

We ate a quiet meal of meatloaf and mashed potatoes. Soft food helped my jaw the most. I finished my coffee. She walked me to the guest room. "I hung some of my ex-husband's old clothes in the closet. They should fit you. I'm across the hall. Don't get any ideas. I'm locking my door."

I slept soundly and woke to an empty house. Kate left coffee for me. I managed to find the toaster for some breakfast. I showered, dressed and watched TV until I fell asleep in a comfortable chair.

Kate ran into the house. "Mac, a man came looking for you at the hospital. A huge man dressed in black, Taz?"

I jumped to my feet. "Do you have a gun in the house?"

"Yes, but I've never used it." She handed me the pistol and a box of bullets. "He won't find you here."

"He might have followed you from the hospital." Suddenly a bullet shattered the front window. I knocked Kate to the floor. The second bullet slammed into the wall over our heads. The only good news, Taz couldn't shoot real well. He relied on his brute strength to punish people. I loaded Kate's gun and crawled to the broken window.

Taz's size made him a very big target. He ran from the oak tree for a closer shot, his fatal error. I could shoot. I did

87

A Story A Day Keeps the EVIL Away

learn something from my brother Gilley. Both bullets hit his chest knocking him backward to the ground. I hurried outside and watched him struggle and bleed in front of me. My last shot went directly into his large head. I took his gun and fished two more clips out of his pocket. Grabbing his Humvee keys, I found Kate standing behind me.

"You're not going back there! They beat you to death last time." Tears welled in her eyes.

"I have to. They nearly killed me twice. I can't wait for them to come after me again." She reached for me. I turned away.

"All you care about is that bitch Isabella!"

I didn't answer. I didn't look back at Kate. I hopped in the Humvee. If they see Taz's vehicle, I might be able to drive right in before they notice. Was I going back for revenge on Gilley or for the love of Isabella? Maybe both. Since I had a couple of hours to drive, I thought about Kate. She had feelings for me. It might be better to turn around and make a new life with her. Sure I've had my share of other women in my life. But Isabella brought a sensual desire I've never known before. Being with her makes the whole world stop. Only the two of us exist in a combination of lust and love. My exotic girl, my reason for living.

Gilley would never understand. He tried to corner the market on beautiful women of every color. Isabella represented his flavor of the month. He would tire of her and send her packing. All I want is one woman, Isabella; he can have the rest for himself.

I crossed into Taver Hts. and knew it would only be twenty more minutes to reach the other side of town and Gilley's house. I had no plans, running on straight adrenaline. Pulling to the side of the street, I reloaded the clip in my gun. Out of

Deadly Desire

the corner of my eye, I saw Taz left a bottle on the floor. I filled my mouth with good Kentucky bourbon. This could be the beginning of my new life or the end of my sorry one. There would be no mercy from Gilley, even for his own brother. I glanced at Joshua's tattoo—DONT COME BACK. Too late. I'm back right now!

Gilley's big country house had a large yard until he bought out his neighbors and tore down their houses. Then he owned the whole street. For late night shipments of guns and drugs, no prying eyes wondered what that truck delivered at four in the morning. At any given moment, six of his henchmen worked in the house or in the vast woods behind the house. Most of the men knew me. I'd work for Gilley off and on. He always overpaid me probably felt sorry for me.

I remember the first time I saw Isabella, the African queen of Gilley's collection of gorgeous, international females. When our eyes met, I knew I had to have her. I started hanging out more at Gilley's house. Unloading trucks, packing boxes, anything to appear useful, I needed to see her, be around her all the time.

That moment in the kitchen her hand touched mine. I reached for her hand squeezing it tightly. This time our eyes locked together for a brief moment. Talk about dangerous desire, my brother's wife! We would exchange words in passing throughout the house.

"He won't let me leave the house ever. I'm like a prisoner here. You know he hits me when he's drunk."

"We have to be careful or he'll kill us both."

Another time days later she said, "I've been putting money aside for us. He'll never miss it."

We stepped into an empty bedroom. I hugged Isabella for

A Story A Day Keeps the EVIL Away

the first time. We shared a passionate kiss. I unbuttoned the front of her white cotton dress. Then I let my hands move across her black skin and she moaned with desire. I had to have her.

"When?" I whispered.

"Tomorrow afternoon, he's leaving with Taz for a meeting downtown. It could take hours."

The next afternoon we planned to take the briefcase of money and leave everything else behind. It didn't happen that way. We were in the bedroom. We were alone in the house. One kiss led to another. Clothes flew in all directions. The blue quilt joined the clothing on the carpeted floor. Passion made its own plans, its own rules. Her perfumed body, her inviting brown eyes, I never heard Gilley's voice until he opened the bedroom door.

Now I approached the house in the Humvee. A red Benz left the four car garage. Seeing my arriving Humvee they assumed a returning Taz and kept the garage door open and honked in my direction. At this time of night, probably a food run before the trucks rolled in again. A lucky break for me. The other two cars in the garage included an emerald green Jaguar and the midnight blue Corvette. Gilley loved his cars. As I closed the garage door, I set the house alarm to warn me when they returned. Any opened door of the house or garage would set it off.

I needed to find Gilley before I could save Isabella and live out my dream life. College football blared from the enormous family room TV sound system. No one occupied the black leather furniture. I entered the adjoining kitchen. There Gilley sat on a bar stool with his back to me. He drank the remainder of his Scotch rocks. "That you Taz? You killed Mac for me?"

"Afraid not Gilley."

He turned to face the pistol I pointed at him. "Don't do

Deadly Desire

anything stupid Mac. You want money, I'll give you money."

"You know what I want, who I want."

"Isabella? She's outta your league brother. She loves me for my money. You have nothing to offer her."

"Is she alright?"

"Outside of that black eye for saying your name, she's perfectly fine." I watched his right hand move slowly to a butcher knife laying on the counter. "You won't leave this house alive. The guys'll kill you if I don't."

"Nice try Gilley. I saw them leave."

He threw his glass at me and grabbed the large knife. My gun fell to the floor. I managed to kick the knife out of his hand. We scrambled for the gun. He elbowed my nose and it exploded in blood. The gun landed across the floor from us. But Gilley moved faster and inched closer to the gun and killing me.

I didn't hear her. Isabella stood over Gilley screaming and stabbing him repeatedly with the butcher knife. Lastly, she buried the knife up to the handle in his back.

Gilley was dead.

"We have to leave now." I pleaded with her. I tossed her a kitchen towel. "Wipe the blood off your hands."

"I need my purse." Isabella hurried up the stairs unsteadily as if the reality of the moment finally caught up with her.

We raced to the Humvee. We'll need different transportation that will blend in soon. I punched in the alarm code and we drove away. With Gilley and Taz both dead we had time to disappear. Isabella sat next to me leaning on my shoulder. Tears of joy and I'm sure regret, streamed down her face. From now on we would live our lives on the run.

By the way, her purse was filled with Gilley's cash!

A Story A Day Keeps the EVIL Away

The Witch's Door

"Hey Jersey Boy, let's go."

"I told ya, call me Mickey. Don't live in Jersey no more." I couldn't stay mad at Ben. He was my first friend in this new country life.

"Where you going son?" Ma's voice from the kitchen. She usually sat at the kitchen table drinking coffee with Aunt Sally and crying 'bout dad. Ma got a folded American flag for daddy. We lost our home and had to move here.

"I'll be back later ma," I called out as I closed the screen door.

"Hey Mickey." Jose joined us. He was younger than me and Ben, but he wanted to hang with us, kinda like a kid brother. Jose wore a navy Yankees cap, probably slept in it too. His messy black hair hung out of his cap and his dark eyes could barely be seen.

"Jose I'm showing Mick that door we found in the woods." Ben stood nearly a foot taller than me and had black-framed glasses that he kept pushing back on his nose. The skinniest and smartest kid I ever met!

A Story A Day Keeps the EVIL Away

"Okay." Jose agreed. He would follow us anywhere.

We walked for what seemed like an hour. "Ain't we there yet Ben?" I asked. We'd been traveling through fields of tall weeds and grass nearly reaching my shoulders. Jose disappeared sometimes. We only saw the top of his Yankees cap.

"Almost there." Ben led the way but stopped when he saw Jose staring at something. We gathered round him. There in front of Jose's face was a fat yellow and black spider showing off its massive web.

"I wanna scoop him up in a jar and take him home." Jose said eagerly.

"Your mother ain't gonna like that Jose. Don't you remember that cool bright red one you found? She gave you a whipping for that spider. Scared hell outta her."

We laughed at the thought of Jose's stern-faced mom screaming 'bout a spider in a jar.

"C'mon guys," Ben suggested and turned towards the woods. The trees were huge and looked like they'd been there forever. Some things were taller than Ben!

"I seen doors before Ben. We go 'em in Jersey too."

"Not like this one."

A few more minutes as we got deeper in the woods, Ben pointed. "See it over there. That black door standing up by itself." We broke into a short run racing to see who would touch the door first.

"Wow!" I exclaimed. The black wooden door had strange, scary carvings. The door was battered by the weather over who knows how many years yet it stood unsupported in front of us. "What do all these things mean Ben?"

Ben pushed his glasses up again and acted like our teacher. "I copied these symbols and went to Mrs. Winslow at the

The Witch's Door

library. She wasn't real happy with the drawings but she gave me this book, "Witchcraft" from behind the counter. And I looked them up."

"You never told me Ben," a disappointed Jose added.

"I didn't wanna scare you Jose. So I'll tell you both." His right arm reached to the large six sided star. "This is used in black magic to bring demons into the world. Ever heard that 666 stuff? This one's got six sides, six points, six small triangles. 666."

I felt myself backing away from the door, from the evil. "I know that one in the middle. It's a goat's head ain't it?"

"Yes Mick. It's connected to the devil." Ben seemed to enjoy scaring me and Jose. "Now this carving on the right that looks like a star inside a circle?"

"Tell us Ben," Jose and I said at the same time.

"Witches used it for their rituals and spells. Bad things like that."

"So a witch lived here Ben?" I put all this new information together to make some sense of the carvings.

"You're right Jersey, I mean Mickey." He took a few steps from the door. "My dad knows…"

"You boys want the real story," a deep voice interrupted. Mallory emerged from the forest. People said he lived in the woods. His shaggy beard and hard face belonged here. Mallory's clothes looked like the forest floor covered in dirt and leaves.

Jose hid behind Ben. "I'm afraid."

"It's okay. Old Mallory wouldn't hurt a fly," Ben reassured him. "You know the story of the witch?"

"Named Mirabella. The legend goes that she disappeared in the woods when she was a child. Woods were deeper then. None of this cutting down trees that happened later. Back in

A Story A Day Keeps the EVIL Away

the 1700s, Mirabella grew up here all alone. One day she cast a spell over two men who built a house for her."

"What happened to her?" I asked.

"Townspeople would visit her in the night for her herbs and potions. Even bought spells from her that brought love or death to others. Most small animals disappeared. No squirrel hunting for many years. The town left Mirabella alone till a little girl, Molly Chambers, vanished after a church picnic. Search parties went through the town and the woods. Then Johnny Warren was missing too."

Jose peeked out. "Did the witch take them?"

"Yes." Mallory continued, "The men of the town swept through the woods carrying torches. They found the witch's house, freed the children and burned the house to the ground with Mirabella inside. She cursed the town and its people screaming through the flames that destroyed her house. The men dug water-filled ditches around the house to keep the forest from burning down. When the fire ended, only the door remained. People said the witch's door was too evil to fall down. You boys stay away from that door. Evil lasts forever."

Just as suddenly as he appeared, Mallory disappeared, blending into the forest again.

I boldly stepped forward. "The door's locked. Wonder what happens if you unlock the door?"

Jose ran behind the door. "You find me on the other side!"

Ben giggled. "The house is gone. Why open the door? What's the point?"

"Don't know. I just wanna open it."

Ben studied the key hole. "I heard 'bout skeleton keys. That's what it'll take. If you really wanna do this Mick, I'll help you find a skeleton key."

The Witch's Door

Jose had a watch and announced, "It's twelve noon. We better head home for lunch." The walk back seemed faster as we talked excitedly 'bout our secret adventure. And the key to the witch's door.

Must have been the next two days Jose and I played video games at his house and caught a baseball with my new glove. "It's a Mickey Mantle glove daddy's favorite player. That's why I'm named Mickey."

"I know who Mickey Mantle was," Jose said.

"Do not Jose. You're too young." When Ben didn't show up for a second day, we went to his house.

"He's not home. Ben went to work with his father," his mother explained.

Jose and I had fun not like when Ben was around. Still, we were happy to see Ben the next morning in front of my house.

"Hey Mick I got it!" Ben shouted.

Jose ran down the street to join us. "Hey where you been?" He brought along his baseball glove and ball.

We wandered in silence waiting for Ben's news. He reached out his left hand opening it to reveal an odd looking key. "It's a skeleton key! We can open the witch's door." Running into the fields we couldn't wait for our new adventure to begin. Jose kept tossing his baseball up in the air and catching it.

"Why'd you bring your glove Jose?"

"Don't know Mickey, just wanted to play catch."

Before long we were leaving the overgrown fields and entering the dark woods. We slowed down when we approached the witch's door. I turned to see Jose's baseball nearly hitting a tree branch until it landed safely in his outstretched mitt.

Ben said, "You should open it Mick. It was your idea." Ben handed me the skeleton key.

A Story A Day Keeps the EVIL Away

"Maybe we shouldn't. Mallory warned us. What if the evil's still there? We could be cursed or something by that dead witch."

Jose chimed in, "Maybe she's not dead."

Ben shook his head. "Look Mickey if you're afraid..."

I cut him off. "Okay I'll do it. Nothing on the other side anyhow."

We all moved forward till we could almost touch the door. Everything seemed to go in slow-motion. I pushed the skeleton key into the lock and turned the key. Jose tossed his baseball into the air. This time the ball bounced off his glove rolling and rolling towards the slowly opening door. Ben reached both of his hands to his glasses. When the door began to move, Ben's glasses broke apart into small pieces of glass floating in the air.

I released the doorknob. It felt like I was holding fire in my hand. A horrible smell filled the air. Blackness greeted my eyes. Then I saw the wrinkled hand reaching out and grabbing Jose as he tried to retrieve his baseball. If that was slow-motion, everything raced to fast-forward. Jose disappeared and the door slammed shut. Ben cried out. I crashed into the closed door but it wouldn't open. Only Jose's Yankee cap remained.

"JOSE, WHERE ARE YOU?" I yelled.

Ben had dropped to his knees holding the frames of his lenses-less glasses. Small cuts from the broken glass marked his face in spots of blood. "Mickey, Mickey, what just happened to me?"

I tried to turn the key again. I tried to save Jose from the witch. Nothing happened. The door refused to move.

"Ben we gotta get help!" I was the leader now. Ben followed me without speaking through the woods, through the fields, and finally onto our street. I never saw Ben cry till that day.

The Witch's Door

"MA, AUNT SALLY HELP!" I screamed as I entered the house. They hurried behind me. Ben's and Jose's mothers joined us.

"Where's my boy? Where's Jose?" His mom cried.

I tried to explain while we ran. I'm sure it sounded crazy to them. I guess some doors should never be opened. We entered the forest. But where was the door? Ben jumped in front of me to lead the way. We scattered searching the woods for the witch's door. Even Mallory aided our search. How could the door that stood alone for hundreds and hundreds of years suddenly vanish?

Perhaps the witch was waiting for one more child to kidnap from the world. With her final victim, poor Jose, the witch disappeared into another realm that we would never find or understand.

Hours, days, weeks the search for Jose lasted into the new school year. But no one ever found Jose.

Ben and I meet every June 17th in the woods reflecting on the day we came face to face with evil. We're adults now but we return every year looking for our long lost friend Jose.

A Story A Day Keeps the EVIL Away

Blood Red Roses

Billy Bob's had a large dance floor but they still moved back tables and chairs. An enormous Confederate flag dominated one wall while an equally huge mirror filled the opposite wall. In the middle of the floor were lines of half-drunk customers stomping their boot heels, clapping, twisting and turning to the blaring country music. "I could use a beer," said everybody when Alan Jackson's "Good Time" ended.

The dark haired beauty emerged from the crowd. Bonnie didn't turn her head knowing the men's eyes followed every move of her hips in her slim cut jeans and every flip of her curly, long black hair. "Let me buy you a drink." Bonnie heard from the male chorus of admirers. Her brown eyes searched for the right one. The tall man shoving the others out of his way reminded her of her ex-Roy, the same cold blue eyes too.

"You honey, you can buy me a beer." Bonnie pulled him forward and kissed his cheek leaving behind hot pink lipstick. His white cowboy hat fell off to the delight of the rejected suitors. He scooped up his hat and walked her to the crowded bar.

"Two drafts Bobby." He yelled over to his friend working

A Story A Day Keeps the EVIL Away

this side of the long bar. "I'm Dewey. Nice to meet you." He stared into her dark brown eyes. "And you are?"

"Call me any name you want cowboy." Bonnie smiled as she hopped on the bar stool. The round of beers came. She finished hers first and looked at Dewey. "That the best you can do cowboy?"

Dewey signaled with two fingers held high. The next beer he gulped down and had a third in his hand. Was this his eighth or tenth beer tonight?

Bonnie's second beer remained untouched in front of her. She leaned towards him exhaling hot breath into his ear, whispering, "Hey sexy let's leave this dump!"

That last beer started to work its magic on his head. Did she really blow into his ear? Damn! "You wanna see my truck honey?"

"This ain't my first rodeo cowboy. I don't wanna see your truck. I wanna see the inside of your truck." Bonnie took off his cowboy hat and threw it towards the far tables. Then she ran her fingers through his brown hair. "C'mon stud!"

Dewey tossed a twenty on the bar. "Bobby, cash me out." She grabbed his arm. This never happened to him. Maybe at last call when he couldn't even tell who he was with. In spite of his good looks he usually went home alone with too much beer in his belly.

The cool night air told Dewey this was really happening. Bonnie pulled apart the pearl buttons on his denim shirt while he fumbled for his keys, dropping them once onto the concrete. Nobody will ever believe me tomorrow at Sam's Lumber. Who cares! Only tonight mattered.

Bonnie pushed his old jacket and several beer cans off the truck's long bench seat. He reached for her kissing her

Blood Red Roses

and kissing her. His long arms pulled her close. Dewey's combined feelings of lust and drunkenness masked the knife blade penetrating his stomach. PAIN? His hand explored the expanding cut. He looked in terror at his blood-covered hand. My god she's gutting me like a fish!

"Don't bleed all over my new jeans asshole!" Bonnie shoved him away. Blood gushed from his gut.

"WHAT HAVE YOU DONE TO ME BITCH?" He fought and lost his battle with consciousness.

"You're just like all men a dumb dead drunk!" Bonnie tossed a long stemmed red rose on the seat. Pulling off her black wig, she crossed the parking lot to her Mazda. Loud rock music kept her awake for the four and a half hour drive over the bridge and into Kentucky. Back to mom's house, her house now. Time to crash for a few hours and deal with life tomorrow morning.

A quick, hot shower helped her cope with the headache that greeted her on mornings like this. Last night's kill was worth it, killing all the Roys in the world. Someday she would murder him, the real Roy.

Bonnie blow-dried and brushed her short strawberry-blonde hair, easy to fit a wig over to hide the real her. The red thong, under black jeans, would make her feel sexy all day. Her matching red bra kept everything in place and prevented them from busting through her long sleeved pink shirt. The contacts! The tinted contacts needed to be replaced and put away for another murderous trip. There, green eyes again reflected back to her in the mirror. Not bad for the other side of thirty!

Meowing came before the grey cat emerged from under the dining room table. "Morning Nelly. Alright I'll feed you." The cat rubbed against her leg. No time for breakfast so she

103

A Story A Day Keeps the EVIL Away

threw together a salad and added a bottle of water for today's lunch.

"The Flower Garden" read the florescent sign in her store window. Opening the front door and shutting off the alarm, Bonnie turned on all the store lights. Besides the visual beauty, the aroma of flowers brought a smile to her face. With her lunch safely in the small refrigerator, she pressed the button on her coffeemaker. She remembered the beautiful roses delivered yesterday before closing.

Pulling out her array of clippers and small scissors, Bonnie placed the first collection of roses on the counter. As the soft rock music played over the ceiling speakers, the Eagles advised her to "Take It Easy." She would. Until the next blood urge wouldn't go away, like last night!

"Morning Bonnie." Like clockwork, William walked in the store. A short man with broad shoulders and hair that resembled an inverted bird's nest. He wore his suit and tie on his way to Lynch Insurance. "How was your trip last night? You should hire a delivery guy. The owner shouldn't be making floral deliveries."

Bonnie clipped the yellow rose and pinned it on the lapel of his suit. "Hi William. This rose complements your navy and yellow striped tie." She kissed him on the lips.

With no response to his questions about deliveries, he asked instead, "What is your favorite color of rose?"

"Blood red."

"Oh yeah. Doesn't that mean love?"

"Yes William." Bonnie needed Clyde, not William. Then she could raise hell robbing banks. Well, maybe not.

He hugged her saying, "Whenever you're ready for the next step in our relationship I'm ready too. You know I dream

Blood Red Roses

about being with you, sleeping with you." She pulled away from his embrace. "I know your ex scared you away from men. I can wait for you Bonnie no matter how long." William smiled sensing the conversation at an end. "I'll call you later Bonnie."

"Bye William. Have a good day." He was naive and probably a virgin, but still a sweet man. Maybe someday she would make his dreams come true, a night he would never forget!

Outside of holidays, her business slowed down especially during the week. Bonnie clipped the remaining roses creating several arrangements. Placing them in the refrigerated display case, her thoughts returned to the cheating husbands who bought many of her roses for their wives or girlfriends. She couldn't prove that Roy cheated on her still he deserved to be called a bastard for many other reasons.

There had been many bruises, a black eye once and many drunken fights where she had tried to hit him too. With her mother's death, she finally had a place to escape from him. Just one more brawl with her violent husband and she would leave him forever.

It happened that weekend getaway at Lake George. Roy brought more alcohol than clothes and spent the entire weekend in various stages of drunkenness, even beer for breakfast! A small argument started over his drinking that led to the last straw for her.

"You've gotta cut back on your drinking Roy."

"Don't tell me what to do! Lay down on the bed."

"You can't do anything when you're this drunk."

Roy backhanded her across the face. Bonnie fell on the bed. "Get away from me!" She screamed. His fist crashed into her nose. Blood exploded all over her face mixing with her tears. He grabbed her flipping her on her stomach. Then he pulled at

A Story A Day Keeps the EVIL Away

her jeans forcing himself on her.

Finally the weight from his body was gone. She staggered to the bathroom and stared at her broken nose, her bloody face and cried. Somehow, she found the strength to call for a cab ride to the hospital. After staying overnight at the hospital, Bonnie asked Carla to drive her back home and stay with her while she took her belongings filling her car and trunk. Then she drove to Miller's Grove, Kentucky to her oasis from pain, her mother's house.

She sold the big diamond from her wedding ring at Regents Jewelry. It became the downpayment on her floral shop. Nine months later, she enjoyed life again. Revenge drove her hours from home for another Roy wannabe to end his life. That brought some satisfaction. But whenever she clipped her lovely red roses, she wanted Roy in front of her, pantless, then snip, snip, snip!

Bonnie reached into her front jeans' pocket—a locket of brown hair crudely cut with her knife last night. A souvenir like the others only what was his name? It started with a D— Dave, Darryl, Dewey, yea Dewey. She stuffed Dewey's hair into a small recipe box in the bottom left drawer. Another blonde hair cutting popped out of the box. Bryan's! Last month Bonnie met that jackass at a wedding reception she crashed. That same cocky attitude and drunken demeanor as old ex-Roy. Bryan wouldn't even wait till they got to his car. Instead he shoved her against the wall of the women's restroom.

Bryan unzipped her alluring little black dress. She drew the sharp knife strapped to her thigh. He died before her dress hit the floor. The quick slash across his neck and Bryan's white shirt and black bow tie turned blood red matching the rose she brought for his dead body. Dressed again Bonnie dragged his

Blood Red Roses

body into a stall and washed her bloody hands. Then she covered the floor with paper towels to soak up the river of blood. A final celebratory drink of champagne, Bonnie toasted her revenge.

No matter how many cold-blooded murders she committed, the face of Roy wouldn't leave her. Empty blue eyes, shaved head, one inch scar by his right eye where another man's ring nearly took his eye in a bar fight, that wicked, unforgiving smile that promised pain to her at any moment. Roy the Rat!

The day passed quickly. Bonnie set the store alarm and drove home. It turned dark early these fall days. As she pulled into her driveway, something was on her front porch. Nelly swinging from a rope with a note attached saying, "YOUR NEXT." Bastard never could spell! My poor cat! She freed the rope from her dead cat. Why did Roy find me after all this time?

There would be no sleep tonight. Bonnie packed an overnight bag. Grabbing her purse, she raced to her car. All the tires were flat! She screamed and ran back into the house. Roy was here! She reached for her cell but a large hand slapped it out of her hand. Bonnie ducked as Roy's powerful punch hit nothing but air. She sprayed mace into his face.

This time he shrieked in pain trying to rub the burning sensation away. Bonnie ran up the stairs. Minutes passed before Roy's blurred vision began to return. Where did she go? Like a wounded animal he knocked over the dining room chairs. "WHERE ARE YOU BITCH? I'M GONNA KILL YOU!"

"Bonnie, what's going on?" William's voice as he entered the house. "Who's this crazy guy?"

Roy grabbed him by his navy and yellow tie and punched him hard knocking him backwards into the dining room wall. Then he kicked William's face. William rolled onto his side

A Story A Day Keeps the EVIL Away

bleeding and in severe pain as he blacked out.

"That's enough Roy!"

Roy turned to face the sawed off shotgun in Bonnie's hands. "You don't know how to shoot that thing. Put it down." Pointing at William he added, "Look I beat up this guy who broke into your house."

"William's his name. Sweet, innocent William. Now I have another reason to kill you!"

Roy rushed towards her reaching for the shotgun. Instead he got the contents of both barrels. Roy's body flew backwards crashing onto the floor. Bonnie spit into Roy's dead face. "Roy you got what you deserved you bastard!"

William opened his eyes to a hospital room filled with multicolored roses. "Bonnie?"

"It pays to date a florist. You have every color of rose from my shop." Bonnie had covered his bed in red rose petals.

"Who was that guy that beat me up?"

"Nobody. He's dead now. Guess I don't need to deliver flowers out of town anymore." She kissed his cheek. "Get better soon William. We need to celebrate and have our special night."

Boxed In

Thanks Uncle Sam! Got his letter in the mail and found out that I'm a 99er. I know I'm not 99 years old. I've heard of the 49ers, San Fran's football team. But 99er was a new term for me, 99 weeks of government assistance. Bottom line, my unemployment checks end today.

    I followed everyone's advice. List three companies out of the phone book on my weekly unemployment form and the checks kept rolling in. Nice gig while it lasted. With a stack of bills coming due, time to pound the pavement and find a real job. What better motivation to go job hunting?

    I kissed Zia goodbye. It would have been more fun to rejoin her in bed. With the classified ad section under my arm, I hopped on the bus for the ride downtown. I marked off a few ads and circled one. Not a lot to choose from. I usually avoided going downtown. An occasional concert or a ball game would draw me there. But downtown also represented jobs. Why is there rush hour traffic during the week? Because everyone is going to work DOWNTOWN! So I'm riding the bus looking for my future employer.

A Story A Day Keeps the EVIL Away

Zia has a red Mustang only she needs her car for her part-time position at Carly's Cuts. Much as I like living with her I never know which Zia would walk in the apartment door. A new style, a new color, hair extensions, Zia tried them all. Could I be cheating on Zia with Zia?

The bus stopped and everyone exited onto public square scattering around the city streets. I opened my newspaper looking for my circled classified ad. Lots of hours, good pay, good benefits for a woman's clothing store, Chic. A small Midwestern chain of stores represented a solid future. Sales to store management? I straightened my tie and walked through Chic's glass doors.

A pretty blonde approached me. "Can I help you sir?"

"Hi. I need to speak to your store manager."

"It's your lucky day." She reached out her right hand. "I'm Linda Manning, the manager at Chic."

I smiled thinking good pay, good benefits and attractive co-workers. I'm all in for this job. "I wanted to apply for the sales associate position."

"Follow me." She led me to her small office in the back of the store. Lots of stylish, colorful clothing on shiny silver racks displayed throughout Chic. Expensive blouses here, dresses there and leather jackets that waited for customers. I sat down in front of her. Time to make a good impression, sound eager and enthusiastic.

I said with a big smile, "I want to work in women's clothing!"

"WHAT?" Linda Manning jumped to her feet. "Are you a cross-dresser or a pervert? Get out of my store! You wear women's clothing somewhere else!"

I ran out of Chic and found myself back on the sidewalk.

Boxed In

That didn't go well!

I glanced at my newspaper again to find my next job offering. "Management training, one position available." As I looked up from the paper, I walked right into a well dressed older European man juggling a Starbucks in one hand and a briefcase in the other. My left hand shot out keeping his coffee from spilling all over his suit. "Sorry," I offered. All I got back from him was The Look.

Brooks Tower stood at the next intersection. I rushed into the huge lobby and found the elevators. The ninth floor doors opened. Let's see room 912 to the right. I stopped at the receptionist's desk. She talked on the phone. I waited for her to look up at me and acknowledge my presence. Instead, she handed me a clipboard and pointed to my left. Twelve others sat filling out applications.

A redhead in a navy pants suit said, "Hi, join the crowd. I'm Doris."

"Jim. Nice to meet you. Anybody called in for an interview yet?"

"No. But the woman across from us has a doctorate in business administration and fifteen years of experience. I've only got a double masters in business and public relations. I'm afraid with eight years in I'll never get the position."

I stood dropping the clipboard on the chair. "I'm in the wrong place. An associate's degree will get laughed at here. Good luck to you."

An early lunch seemed like my first good idea of the day. When I entered Burger King, I saw a sign for "counter help." Did I dare ask? A perky young girl in her uniform said, "Can I take your order?"

"That sign for counter help?"

111

A Story A Day Keeps the EVIL Away

She whispered, "Don't even ask. Our manager's a real bitch. Trust me you don't wanna work here."

I placed my order and walked off with my plastic tray to an empty table. Munching on some fries, I called Zia on my cell. "Hope your day's better than mine."

"Hi Jim. I'm leaving for the shop in a few minutes. No luck honey?"

"Nothing. There is a long shot in the classifieds. Guess I'm desperate enough to stop there after lunch. I feel like a one-legged man in a butt kicking contest."

She laughed. "Glad you haven't lost your sense of humor. Leftover pasta for dinner later?"

"Sounds good Zia. See you soon." I finished my burger. One more look at the classified ad section led my eyes to the bottom of the page. "Up to the challenge? One week of pay guaranteed. Holiday Inn conference room B." Why not?

I walked two blocks and crossed the street to the Holiday Inn. Passing through the lobby, I followed signs to the conference rooms. I entered conference room B. Two people sat at a long table facing the door. An attractive brunette with green eyes smiled at me. But the surprise was the second person. The same older man I crashed into on the sidewalk. No pleasant reception from him.

I froze and considered leaving the room.

"Please have a seat. My name is Annabel and this is my father Edgar."

I sat. "I'm Jim Whitmore. Happy to meet you both." Edgar stared at me with an expressionless face. Had he forgotten about our accidental encounter?

"Just a few questions for you Mr. Whitmore," Annabel continued. "Are you a reliable person?"

Boxed In

"Yes."

"Are you someone who can follow directions and keep secrets from others?"

"As long as it's legal, I'm your man."

Annabel said to Edgar, "I have a good feeling about this one father." He nodded but didn't speak. "We will give you five hundred dollars and a box. You need to have the box with you at all times. In twenty-four hours you will return the box unopened and receive an additional five hundred dollars. Then we will decide whether or not to offer you full time employment at a high salary. Please write down your basic information on this application."

Annabel counted out five one-hundred dollar bills. Reaching inside a large black bag, she placed a silver box, the size of a woman's shoe box, on the table next to the money. Handing her back the completed application, I stood in front of her. Annabel extended the money and box to me. "Best of luck Mr. Whitmore. We will see you tomorrow morning."

I stuffed the money deep in my pocket. Next I tucked the box tightly under my arm. "Thanks for giving me this chance." Edgar watched me leave the room without saying a word.

Checking the bus schedule, I ran to public square hoping to catch the next bus. As I passed a group of people exiting the bus, did I see a woman wearing a jean jacket and carrying a silver shoe box?

"You getting on the bus or what buddy?" The burly driver yelled at me.

"Sorry." I climbed up the steps and found a seat in the back. Two identical boxes? I stared out the window. Was this some sort of test with the winner getting the job? I twisted my neck following a third person also carrying a silver box walking

113

A Story A Day Keeps the EVIL Away

down the sidewalk. How many silver boxes existed?

I daydreamed about having a good job and joining the rest of the working world. I guess I've watched too many TV commercials. Everybody in those commercials always seems happy with their perfect lives, perfect houses, three perfect kids and a new car in the driveway. Does anybody really live like that?

Then I stared at the silver box in my lap. It appeared to be sealed. When I lifted it, there was no shake, rattle or roll sound from the box. I could tell the box weighed more than an empty box. The mysterious contents remained hidden.

I left the bus at Western and Ridge proceeding down the street to my high-rise apartment building. Actually, Zia found the apartment for us. A simple two bedroom but we needed the second bedroom to store all our combined junk. Of course my parents' attic held the remainder of my possessions.

While I waited for Zia to return, I checked our Chores List on the refrigerator, dishes for me. I washed a few mugs and piled the rest into our small dishwasher. I nearly jumped out of my shoes when a loud knocking came from the apartment door. The peephole revealed nothing useful. I kept the chain on and opened the door.

A large man in a tan trench coat demanded, "Give me the box! Don't get wise with me I know you got it!"

"What are you talking about?"

"The silver box. I don't wanna hurt you." I knew he could do serious damage to my body.

"Go away or I'll call the police!" I bluffed.

"Name's Nichols. I'll be back." He skipped the elevator heading for the stairs.

Am I in a James Bond movie? I looked out the window and watched Mr. Nichols emerge from the apartment building. He

Boxed In

joined another man seated in a dark sedan across the street. Guess I was lost in thought and I didn't hear Zia trying to open the door.

"Jim, why do you have on the chain lock?"

"I forgot." I removed the chain and greeted her with a quick kiss.

"Like today's hair, strawberry blonde?" She giggled knowing I hated her daily changes.

"Did you notice anything odd when you parked your car?"

"Some guy in a trench coat yelled across the street, 'It's not her.'"

"Nobody could ever identify you from one day to the next."

Zia walked past me and picked up the silver box. "You bought me new shoes! How thoughtful!"

"Don't open it!" I snatched the box from her hands. "That's my good news and bad news. I've got a job but there are men outside that will use physical force to acquire that box."

"Just give it to them. It's not worth a trip to the hospital."

"Let's wait till dark and then we'll make our move." I explained everything to Zia over our leftover pasta dinner. After placing five one hundred bills on the kitchen table, she agreed to my plan.

I glanced out the window and saw a third trench coated man. Must have got a great deal on trench coats. This guy was plump, to be kind to him. Let's put it another way, if he played Santa Claus no extra padding would be needed. He talked to the men in the car and disappeared from sight, probably the guy from the parking lot.

I called the Holiday Inn downtown and made a reservation for tonight. Now we had to get there safely with the silver box. "Okay Zia, you leave first. Pull your car up to the back exit." She

A Story A Day Keeps the EVIL Away

left with a small suitcase. A typical overnight for her included two suitcases and three shoe boxes. Her excuse? "I never know what I'm gonna wear." Five minutes later with my overnight bag and the silver shoe box, I rode the elevator to the first floor. Outside Zia's red Mustang waited for me. But the trench coat guy saw me too.

The fat man ran or waddled screaming, "It's Whitmore! It's Whitmore!" I was surprised he could move that fast without a box of donuts encouraging his flight. Before he reached the others, we pulled into traffic. At times like this, I wish Zia's car was any color but red, too easy to spot.

Danica Patrick would be proud of Zia's driving. Zooming in, out, and around cars we arrived downtown and drove into Holiday Inn's underground parking garage. Instead of Jim Whitmore, Zia signed in using her name at the registration desk. Then we agreed not to answer the door to anyone.

I woke up amazingly without an overnight confrontation from the trench coat guys. We dressed and hurried to the lobby with the silver box. Opening the conference room door, Annabel, Edgar and the three trench coats were all there waiting for us.

I turned to leave until Annabel reassured me. "It's alright. You're safe. Please sit down." We pulled up chairs. "Congratulations, you are the winners!"

In front of us rested five silver boxes on the table. I said wearily, "Please explain these other boxes. What's going on here?"

"We gave out six boxes," Annabel began. "Then we hired these men to find the boxes and return them to us any way they could. Some boxes were bought. Others were stolen. You have the only box left."

Boxed In

"You tested me?"

"Yes." Edgar spoke up for the first time. "I remember our initial meeting on the sidewalk. You impressed me with your manners and your reactions. You saved my suit from a trip to the cleaners."

"Here is your contract with us. I am sure you will be happy with all the zeroes." Annabel handed me an envelope.

"I have to ask—what was in the silver boxes?"

"Pages from the phone book. Nothing of value. You passed the test and you are now part of our team!"

A Story A Day Keeps the EVIL Away

Junior

PART 1

The pillow flew across the bedroom striking Julie in the back as she zipped her grey skirt. "Come on back to bed. We're celebrating your divorce!" Sully sat in his boxers dangling his legs onto the floor. "There's still champagne left from last night."

Julie turned to face him. She did love him but Sully needed to hear the truth. "Take a shower. You'll be late again. Collins is ready to suspend you." Julie slipped on her matching grey jacket. "And my divorce was final last week."

"You don't need me at the police station. You said there's been no murders for the past two weeks."

"Do I have to say the name? Willa? She's dead." Willa's brutal murder would not leave them even now. "It's time to move on with your life." Julie's brown eyes locked into Sully's blue eyes. "If you want me to be part of your life, it's up to you. I don't wanna be a rebound girl." She checked her blonde hair in the mirror one last time. "I'm leaving. Hurry up!"

Julie drove halfway to the station lost in her thoughts

A Story A Day Keeps the EVIL Away

when her cell rang. "We knew our luck would end. What's the address lieutenant? I'll tell Sully to meet us. He'll be there; he's just running late today." She texted Sully's cell with all the details.

An empty warehouse that had the reputation for drug activity became the center of attention. Covering her shoes, Julie entered the crime scene. She found Ray kneeling over the dead body. The white male appeared to be in his forties. She looked at what remained of the victim's face and turned her head away. It reminded her of that first crime scene as a detective with dead bodies and blood everywhere.

Ray glanced up. "Good morning Julie. Hell of a way to start the day. We've got a single bullet to the head, nearly took his face off. Needle marks on both arms. Probably a drug deal gone bad. Heroin's taking over the streets again."

A tall gangling young man approached them. "Got the shell casing dad." He wore a bright red bow tie with his white shirt. His short black hair was spiked.

Julie stood. "You're Ray's son? I'm Detective Julie Francis. Call me Julie. Nice to finally meet you."

Ray rose from the floor. "He's Raymond Junior but Martha and I have called him Junior his whole life. Still lives with us."

Junior smiled. "Hi Julie. I'm trying to learn from the best forensics guy around, my dad."

Sully walked up to them. "Your boy Ray?" He reached out his right hand. "Detective Sullivan, just Sully is fine. Welcome to the worst job in the world. Whatever war stories your dad's told you about this job, they're all true." Sully compared the short, stocky bald headed Ray to Junior and added, "Looks more like the mailman than you Ray."

"Come with me Sully," Ray said grabbing his arm. "Let's

Junior

talk outside."

They reached the large parking lot. "What's the matter Ray? Can't take a joke?"

Ray couldn't control his anger. "I can smell the alcohol on your breath from here! Get your head outta your ass! Julie's been covering for you the past few weeks. Everyone knows you're drinking all the time. You're not fooling anybody, including Collins."

Sully stared down at his shoes. "It's Willa, I..."

"Everybody loses someone," Ray cut him off. "It happens to all of us. Nearly a month has gone by. People are counting on you. You've been a great detective. We need you back."

Sully donned his sunglasses. The early morning sun made his perpetual headache worse. Ray was right of course. But...

A speeding car, bullets flying towards them. Sully reached for his pistol and dropped it on the pavement. Ray knocked him off his feet as bullets sprayed the parking lot. Then it ended. Red blood decorated his black suit, not his blood. Ray had been hit multiple times.

People ran from the warehouse at the sound of gunfire. Ray gasped for breath. An ambulance already headed to the warehouse rushed over with paramedics. Sully walked away from the gathering crowd. He had to clear his head. Details, he needed details about the car, about the shooter.

PART 2

Mulligan's restaurant and bar had two patrolmen finishing breakfast when Detective Sullivan found a table in the back. He held his head in his hands. *Did I get Ray killed?* Sully kept talking to himself.

"Little early for a drink," Mulligan said. He looked fifty

A Story A Day Keeps the EVIL Away

but really approached seventy. A former police detective who had been injured on the job went on disability and opened a cop bar. "Damn Sully! You got blood all over your suit! Rough morning. How 'bout a cup of strong coffee?"

"Yea, thanks. I'll need more than one cup." He closed his eyes and focused on the speeding car. Dark sedan, Buick? Tinted windows. One driver, one shooter. Not after Ray. They were after me! Sully smelled the coffee before he saw it. Two large sips later, his mind returned to the shooter.

Long dark hair, black framed glasses, Mexican cartel. Name? A hired gun from out of town. He's been here other times. Where and when? The name, the name was Carlos Cabrera. A cartel hit man taking a contract on one Detective Sullivan.

Sully downed his coffee nearly burning his mouth. He raced to the counter handing over a five dollar bill. "Throw in those breath mints Mully. Thanks."

A fast pace walk led him into the police station. He chewed a handful of mints. Julie greeted him, "Ray's in critical condition. Fortunately, the bullets managed to miss his vital organs. There's surgery scheduled to remove three bullets. Ray lost a lot of blood."

"Thanks for the update." Before he took another step, Lt. Collins hurried to his side.

"You've got some explaining to do!" Collins barked at him. "Where's your report on Ray's shooting? What do you remember?"

"Give me a minute to write it down. We need an APB on Carlos Cabrera. He's the shooter. I'd start with airports, bus terminals. They'll want him out of town."

Julie followed Sully to his desk. "What have you got on

Junior

the car?"

"Buick, dark color, tinted windows, New York plates."

"I'll run it through to the patrol cars in the warehouse district." She paused and asked, "Are you okay?"

"Just needed a kick in the ass from Ray. I thought he was DOA."

Julie left and Sully wrote his report. As he rose from his desk, he saw a man running in his direction, Ray's son?

Lt. Collins reached him first. "Hold on Junior!"

"My dad almost died because of that man!"

"Not true son." Collins led him into his office closing the door.

Julie returned to Sully's desk. "A patrol car found that Buick abandoned over on Riverside. Reported stolen. Nothing inside the car."

"You missed Junior. Collins intercepted him on his way to me. Blames me for his dad's shooting." Sully sat and clicked on his computer. "Let's see...Carlos Cabrera." Carlos's picture appeared with his arrest record. "Wanted by the FBI, MI6, Interpol, he's got a full dance card. Carlos must have a good lawyer. He's only been in prison four-and-a-half years."

"I recall the prosecution witnesses disappearing or ending up dead."

Lt. Collins walked over as Junior glared in Sully's direction before leaving the station. "AK-47 assault rifle. You're lucky to be alive."

"Ray saved my life." Sully responded. "I want to go over to Memorial Hospital but I don't know how Martha and Junior will react."

"Sully, you need a low profile. I've thought about your shooter. He never leaves till his target is dead. Carlos never left;

123

A Story A Day Keeps the EVIL Away

he's still here." Collins advised.

Julie said to Sully, "I'll go to the hospital with you. I want to be there during the surgery. Several policemen gave blood already."

"The two of you be careful." Collins watched them leave.

PART 3

Sitting in Memorial Hospital's waiting room, Carlos Cabrera held the USA TODAY in front of his face. His long hair was tucked under a wool cap. Sunglasses replaced the black frames. Sullivan would show up. Carlos waited for his target to arrive.

Sully and Julie hurried through the waiting room to the elevators. With all the violence surrounding police officers, they knew surgery took place on the third floor with a separate waiting area. As the elevator doors began to close, a single shot rang out missing Sully's head by inches. The second bullet ricocheted off the closing elevator doors.

Pressing the Open button repeatedly, the elevator doors opened again. Sully and Julie rushed into the waiting room with guns drawn. The room was empty. Two hospital security guards ran into the room. Sully flashed his gold detective shield to the men. The security guards followed Sully through the entrance doors onto the sidewalk. An elderly couple stopped in terror in front of them before continuing to the entrance. Nobody else appeared.

Finally, Sully and Julie reached the third floor. Martha greeted them with long hugs. But Junior kept his distance. Sully sat next to Junior. "I know you're mad at me. The truth is your father saved my life. He pushed me to the ground."

"Thought you were a great detective," Junior responded through clenched teeth. "Why didn't you protect my dad?"

Junior

"It happened too fast," Sully tried to forget his pistol slipping from his hand when he could have stopped them. "We know the shooter. We'll bring him to justice."

They waited quietly with Julie buying coffees after the second hour passed. Sully started pacing unable to remain seated, staring at the clock that barely moved. At last the surgeon, Dr. Albers, walked directly to Martha.

"He's stable. Removing the third bullet by his spine took most of the last hour. He'll be in recovery for awhile. Martha, Ray's gonna be fine."

Sully noticed someone standing behind him. He spun around and looked down. A hand reached up to his. "Kaiko Suzuki to protect you." A smiling Japanese man shook his hand. Before Sully could speak or react, Junior approached him.

Junior's second foot barely touched the floor when Kaiko leaped into action. Suddenly, Junior's body flew into the air and crashed onto the carpeted floor. "OW!" Junior cried in pain.

"Nobody touch Detective Solly!" Kaiko stood over him. A shocked Sully helped Junior to his feet.

"He's not a threat to me," Sully explained.

"Name is Kao okay?" The well dressed man bowed slightly to Sully. "Collins sent me to you."

"This is Julie," Sully introduced her. "Don't harm her either. She's on our side."

"Protect her body too," Kao responded with a laugh.

"You've been briefed on Cabrera?"

"The bad guy. Tried to shoot Solly."

"Sully!"

"Solly."

"Whatever." Sully gave up. "We've got to leave. Martha, Ray Junior take care. We'll be in touch." Julie hugged Martha

A Story A Day Keeps the EVIL Away

before they headed to the elevator.

The elevator doors opened. Julie jumped back in shock. "Oh my god!" The two hospital security guards were stacked one on top of the other. Both had been shot multiple times.

"We're gonna need an army just to get outta the hospital." Sully said reaching for his phone.

"I one-man army," Kao replied bravely. As they climbed down the stairs to the lobby, Kao added, "I drive too. Your keys Solly."

PART 4

Detective Sullivan marveled at Kao's driving. "Impressive! I think you've watched too many Japanese action movies." The car weaved through traffic. "Carlos is out here somewhere." Sully stared through the car windows.

A black car emerged approaching the driver's side, Sully's side. The back window shattered. Sully returned fire. Julie ducked reaching for her pistol. Sully's third shot missed Carlos but hit the driver's head. The black car spun sideways. A body tossed out of the car. The driver's dead body hit the pavement as Carlos gained control of the car and disappeared into traffic.

Kao was boxed in by other cars and couldn't continue the chase. He muttered something in Japanese banging his hands on the steering wheel. Nobody asked Kao to translate his angry words.

They safely reached the police station. Collins met them saying, "Ray Junior joined the investigation at Memorial. Understand you had a problem on the road."

"Carlos threw his driver out of the car in the middle of traffic." Julie explained.

"Did we get prints on the driver?" Sully asked.

Junior

"They'll be processed within the hour." Collins walked with them. "I see you've met your new bodyguard. Kao came in from the Metro office. He knows the city and will help keep you safe."

"Carlos isn't gonna stop till one of us is dead." Sully became angry, "Instead of him chasing me, I need to find him and kill him!"

"We're not vigilantes. Everyone is allowed his day in court." Collins whispered to Sully, "Off the record, if you kill him, nobody will miss him. The FBI will be here tomorrow and take over the investigation of Cabrera. We have twenty-four hours to find him and put him down."

"I'll make some calls." Julie said. "One of my informers may be able to help us."

Sully and Kao sat in Collins' office. Collins continued, "You probably didn't know but Kao commanded all the citywide security when the presidential candidates visited here. He's well respected throughout the department. I borrowed him for a few days."

"I can't just sit around," Sully said rising to his feet. "Carlos isn't gonna walk in here."

"Be patient. If Carlos's people are watching the station, maybe we can set them up with a decoy. I'll need your help Kao." Kao nodded to Collins.

Julie entered saying, "Carlos has been spotted around Liberty City, Angel Santiago's bar. It would be a good place to start. We've investigated there before."

Collins said, "Take a couple patrolmen with you. I need Sully and Kao with me."

Julie followed the patrol car through the streets to Liberty City.

A Story A Day Keeps the EVIL Away

"You get the special car Kao." Collins searched his desk for the keys. "It's an unmarked sedan with bulletproof glass. Take Tony Brooks with you. He's about Sully's height and build."

Collins led Sully to his car and alerted the closest patrol cars of his plans. They waited for Kao's car, keeping a safe distance behind. Collins noticed two cars start to gain on Kao.

Kao zoomed through a red light. Cars hit their brakes and their horns, except the two cars that continued the chase. Collins yelled over his radio, "Close it down now!" Patrol cars flew in from all directions. Kao swerved turning his car directly into the path of the attacking cars.

Using the car doors for protection, Kao and Tony opened fire as police cars closed down the surrounding streets. Two men jumped from one of the cars hands in the air. But Carlos came out firing. One officer fell in the gunfire. Kao aimed and fired. The single shot exploded into Carlos's chest. He died instantly falling on the pavement.

Sully and Collins ran over to the dead body of Carlos Cabrera. Kao smiled. "I shoot good too!"

"I've got a call to make," Sully said as he walked to the sidewalk. "Raymond Junior, it's Detective Sullivan. The shooter has been killed. I thought you'd want to know."

"Thanks detective. I talked to dad for a few minutes. He's pretty weak from the surgery. He wanted you to know that I'll be the new lead forensics guy. Dad's retiring."

"Well say hi to your dad. Guess we'll be working together soon. By the way, get rid of that bow tie."

April Fooled

"It's over. Let's call off the wedding."

Julie searched Sully's handsome face. All the years they'd known each other had led to this? Tears formed in the corners of her soft brown eyes. "Sully..."

"April Fool's honey!" His wide smile didn't chase away her tears.

"You are a cruel man!" Finally she returned his smile. "We are getting married tomorrow. No more jokes today." She looked around the kitchen. "Where is my purse? I have to leave."

"In the refrigerator of course." Sully laughed. "I've gotta make a stop on the way. Received a text from an old friend in trouble."

Sully drove to the crime scene flashing his gold shield at the police officers. Another cheap motel, Johnson's Inn, rented by the hour in the red light district. No tell motels where husbands came to cheat on their wives with women of the night. Johnson's Inn had its share of crimes from soliciting to murder.

Sully entered to the sight of a dead man wearing only

A Story A Day Keeps the EVIL Away

boxers over his big stomach face down on the carpet by the bed. Raymond Junior kneeling over the body commented, "Why are you here Sully? It's not a homicide probably a heart attack for Charles Braddock of Brooklyn."

"Where's Venus?" Sully asked.

"Here Sully." The tall black female answered wearing her red Victoria's Secret working attire. Her long, curly black hair had royal blue streaks. "They won't let me leave. I gave them my statement. I even called 911 for John or whatever his real name is."

"Let's talk in the bathroom." She followed him. "So what happened?"

"White man got too excited when he saw these black beauties," she said removing her red bra.

"Very nice, now put them away Venus."

"New implants Sully, practically pay for themselves." She stepped towards him. "Touch 'em they won't bite."

"Thanks but no thanks. I'm getting married tomorrow." Sully revealed.

"Back in the day I never had to ask you twice." She produced her sexiest smile. "Why don't you close the door and I'll give you a wedding present?"

"Let's get you outta here." Sully resisted the offer and returned to the bedroom crime scene. He announced, "Venus is free to go. The only thing dangerous about her is her body." Laughter erupted as he left the room.

Sully met the paramedics when they exited the ambulance. He handed them a piece of paper, two twenty dollar bills, and his card. They parted giggling over Sully's directions.

When Sully reached the station, Julie left Lieutenant Collins' office. She greeted him with a warm kiss. "Collins told

April Fooled

me to take the whole day off because of our wedding. I have some paperwork to finish then it's off for my hair and nails appointment."

"That reminds me I still gotta pick up my tux." Before she could respond, he added, "I picked it up yesterday. It's hanging in the closet."

"Always the kidder." She stood by his desk. "Who was your urgent call this morning?"

"Venus the hooker. Had a dead John."

"I busted her before when I worked vice. Nice girl in the wrong profession."

"America's oldest profession."

"I've got work to do." Julie walked back to her desk.

Sully flipped through a stack of folders on his desk. All of the unsolved murders tied to the serial killer targeting prostitutes. No evidence and no witnesses. The body count stood at seven. He should have warned Venus. But in her world, bad news traveled fast.

The desk phone rang. He answered, "Detective Sullivan, how can I help you?"

"I need your advice."

"Who is this?"

"Raymond Junior. Sully, the body from this morning disappeared! It never arrived at the morgue! What'll I do? They'll fire me for sure!"

"Why didn't you call your father with all his years of experience working crime scenes?"

"My parents are on vacation in Florida. I don't wanna bother them. Sully, what should I do?"

"Calm down Junior. I'll make some calls and get back to you when I hear something."

131

A Story A Day Keeps the EVIL Away

"Thanks Sully. I owe you."

Laughing, Sully hung up the phone. How long should he let Junior sweat it out before he told him April Fool's? Maybe after lunch.

This time his cell rang. "Sully."

"It's me Venus." She could barely speak.

"Don't tell me you're in trouble again!"

"Not me Sully, my white girl Vanessa. She's dying. I got blood all over my hands. It's that serial killer! He sliced her up!"

"Where are you?"

"Seventeenth and Madison. The old Merchant Hotel. Hurry Sully!"

Putting the flashing red globe on his car, Sully's car flew through the morning traffic. Police cars blocked off the street. Showing his detective shield, he was waved through to the front of the hotel. Sully ran up the steps stopping at the third floor. Several policemen waved or nodded in his direction.

"Hooker said she'll only talk to you." A patrolman led him to the bedroom. Vanessa's nude body lay on the bed with her throat slashed. Her bleach blonde hair turned red from the growing pool of blood surrounding her head. Venus rushed into his arms crying. Her soiled hands made their red marks on his blue shirt and navy suit.

Sully hugged her asking, "Why were you here Venus?"

"John wanted a threesome. Offered lots of cash. Vanessa called me and described him to me. I was late 'cause of this morning or me and Vanessa both be dead."

"Let's wash up in the bathroom."

She scrubbed the blood from her hands and arms still in tears. Then she noticed the red blood all over Sully's clothes in the mirror. "Oh I'm sorry. Didn't mean to ruin your suit."

April Fooled

Ignoring her comment, Sully questioned, "You said Vanessa told you what the killer looks like?"

"That's right, trying to talk me into working with her on the dude. Write this down Sully." He pulled a small notebook from his suit coat pocket.

"Go ahead Venus."

"One condition and I'm serious Sully. I get to ride along with you and find the bastard!"

"Now Venus, you know..."

She cut him off saying, "He can't be more than twenty, thirty minutes ahead of us. Vanessa was like a sister to me. Please Sully, you know I'd do anything for you."

"Okay, we'll leave together but I need his description."

"Probably mid-thirties, dark hair, full beard covering a long scar on his face. Tattoos on his arms and hands. Likes wearing sleeveless shirts to show off his tatts."

Venus followed Sully down the stairs to his car. A patrolman yelled out, "You her pimp Sully?" The other officers laughed; Sully never turned his head. Nothing funny about the eighth dead prostitute with a killer on the loose.

"Lots of working girls in the bars round here. Lemme talk to them," she offered. They drove into the neighborhoods where even the police weren't comfortable and looked over their shoulders at the gathering of ex-cons, gang members and drug addicts in the bars. Sully parked on the street and let Venus lead the way.

"Why you here girl? This ain't your turf!" Two prostitutes got in her face until Sully appeared next to her.

"Chill. Lookin for a killer. Remember Vanessa hangs with me sometimes? Girl's dead got her throat cut wide open. You seen a guy tattoos and dark beard?"

A Story A Day Keeps the EVIL Away

"No honey. Text you if we do."

Two more bars and nothing but potential police lineups for various crimes in the future. "I've gotta get back to the station and post an APB on our suspect's description."

"Sully, cross the street. That guy lighting up a smoke. Could be that sick bastard." Before Sully reacted, she ran over and confronted him.

"YOU KILLED VANESSA!"

Sully reached her and saw the flash of metal, a knife. Tossing away his cigarette, the killer held the knife on Venus' throat. "Back off cop or whoever you are. I'm taking her to my car."

"Drop the knife!" Sully screamed as he hurried towards them.

"Nothing but a two bit whore! I'm gonna kill 'em all, clean these city streets."

Sully leveled his pistol at the man's head. "Last warning punk! Drop the knife!"

Venus's right stiletto heel kicked straight back into his groin. He hollered in pain and collapsed on the sidewalk dropping the knife harmlessly in front of him. Sully quickly cuffed him, kicking away the knife.

"We make a great team Sully. Admit it."

Sully nodded requesting a squad car. Then he said to Venus, "Those red heels of yours are deadly weapons! And yes, we were a great team. You need to come back to the station and give a written statement."

After reading him his rights, Sully shoved the killer into the waiting patrol car. Then they drove back to the police station.

"My desk is kinda messy. Let's use the conference room Venus." He found a legal pad of paper and pen handing it to her as she sat down. "Just write your statement starting with

April Fooled

Vanessa's phone call to you."

Seeing a red-faced man in a white shirt and orange bow tie, Sully ran to meet him. "Sully, don't try to talk me out of resigning! Charles Braddock's body was my responsibility. I'm taking my letter to Collins." Junior walked even faster.

Detective Sullivan gripped him by the shoulders. "Slow down! I tracked the body to the East District's morgue. It will be returned this afternoon."

Junior hugged him tightly. "Thank you, thank you so much! You saved my career. Dad would have been embarrassed."

"Yea," Sully said pulling away. "And April Fool's Junior." He hurried from Junior as the red-faced look returned.

Lt. Collins left his office. "What's all the commotion about?"

"Nothing, a misunderstanding sir." Junior replied as he marched angrily to the elevator.

"Sully, there's someone I want you to meet." Collins was joined by a well-dressed African American man. "Detective Sullivan, this is our newest detective. Got his gold shield this morning, Russell Gibbs."

They shook hands. "Call me Sully."

"What happened to your suit?" Gibbs asked.

"Don't worry. It's not my blood. Occupational hazard. I'm sure you know what happens on our city streets." Sully compared the two men and observed, "Lieutenant, he looks like you ten years ago. Your long lost younger brother?"

"No." Collins laughed. "He'll probably have my job one day. Russell will pick up some of the caseload with Julie and you on your honeymoon." Collins turned to Gibbs. "You'll learn a lot from Sully. He closed a serial killer case that's been open for weeks."

"The lessons start after my honeymoon cruise. Nice

135

A Story A Day Keeps the EVIL Away

meeting you. I've gotta finish taking a witness' statement."

Venus greeted him by saying, "You give me that dry cleaning bill Sully. Gotta let me do that for you if you don't wanna enjoy my payment options." That stay with me tonight smile had drawn him in many times but not with his marriage to Julie waiting for him tomorrow.

"Don't you worry Venus," Sully reassured her, "I got this guy downtown who gives me free dry cleaning for killing the man who raped and murdered his wife." He paused adding, "If you had waited a split second before using your heel, I'd have blown his head off his shoulders."

Venus smiled at the bloody vision. "You the devil alright. My kinda devil!"

Saturday morning brought overcast skies and potential for showers. Sully searched the radar on his cell. "There looks like a break in the storms this afternoon, just like I planned it. Perfect wedding weather."

"That's why I booked the outdoor chapel." Julie kissed his cheek. "Now you take your tux and go let Collins buy you breakfast at Mulligan's. I'll see you later for the big moment!"

Red roses climbed the trellis around the white gazebo. Fifty wooden chairs were scattered in front and filled by the wedding guests, including Venus in her one acceptable "church dress." Sully stood in a black tuxedo with Michael Collins standing beside him.

The music played. People watched Julie in a floor-length ivory dress with her long blond hair clipped on top of her head. She joined Sully. The smiling pastor spoke, "Do you…"

"We both do." Sully interrupted, taking Julie in his arms and kissing her.

A Gift for Santa

I placed another log on the fire and felt the warmth fill the family room. My son Ted struggled to tear the Santa wrapping paper from his big Christmas present. My lovely wife Mary left the glow of the fireplace and knelt down in her red nightgown to aid Ted in his efforts. The smell of pine complemented the taste of eggnog in my reindeer glass. I paused for a moment taking a mental picture of Mary and Ted with the enormous, decorated Christmas tree behind them. A beautiful holiday memory!

But then I opened my eyes to the reality of a small apartment, a tiny Christmas tree and no Mary or Ted, just like it's been for four years now. I was between jobs, which is nothing new. Fortunately, I waited for a phone call that would provide me with seasonal employment.

I opened the refrigerator and found the usual: generic beer in white cans (Bob's Beer?), generic cola, white bread a week past the expiration date, lunch meat I can't identify, the cheese with the holes—Swiss, and a freezer full of microwave dinners. At least the rent's paid for December and the electric bill too.

A Story A Day Keeps the EVIL Away

Gotta TV outta the trash my neighbor Ray threw out. It works good enough. Ray got one of those HD big screen TVs. No cable for me either. Maybe someday.

My cell phone rang. "Bobby, Bobby Richards?"

"Yes sir that's me."

"This is Mr. Masters the store manager at Watkins Department Store. It's Christmas time again. We would like to offer you a job as our store Santa Claus starting on Wednesday."

"Thanks Mr. Masters. I would love to work for you."

"Good Bobby. I'll see you Wednesday nine o'clock sharp."

I'll have money for the holiday season. I owned one Christmas decoration a small Christmas tree that has seen better days. I kept it in my apartment storage space till December. Sometimes the little lights blink and other times they don't. They usually stayed on in all their bright colors.

Wednesday came and I set two alarms so I wouldn't sleep too late. I took the Grant Street bus which stopped right across the street from Watkins Department Store. The Santa job barely paid over minimum wage but they gave me a cafeteria pass good for one meal each day as long as I worked there. You better believe I loaded my tray at the department store cafeteria. And good food too, better than my cooking.

The store dry cleaned the Santa suit before December. It had two pairs of pants which came in handy sometimes. I tried the red suit on and it fit fine. It seemed like every year I required less and less padding. Guess that said a lot for my physically unfit body!

Jingle bells announced my arrival. I entered Candy Cane Lane on my way to the "North Pole." Large red and white candy canes and huge Christmas trees decorated each side of my Santa throne. My boots walked across the fluffy fake snow as

A Gift for Santa

the children in line screamed and several jumped up and down. The padded seat on my Santa throne didn't help much by the end of the day.

The Keller twins, Bev and Becky, dressed in their cute green elf costumes with green hats. The two blonde college juniors have been working here since high school. They filled their green outfits the right way, not like me and my Santa suit. Sure I looked at them. It helped the day pass faster.

"Bev, bring the first child up," I said.

"It's Becky, Santa."

"Sorry." I always mixed them up.

The first little girl wore a white sweater with a red reindeer over her designer jeans. She jumped on my lap and started talking before I did. "Hi Santa. Mom and I sent you an email with all the toys I really want. Can you get something nice for mom like diamonds? She loves diamonds."

"I'll see what I can do honey. Merry Christmas." Bev, or was it Becky, gave her a candy cane while her sister brought the next boy to me. "Merry Christmas. What would you like for Christmas?"

His navy Dallas Cowboy sweatshirt seemed too large for him. "I'm on your naughty list Santa. My mom had a baby, baby sister and I don't help her. I've been a brat. But if I could have a puppy, I know my sister would like it too." He pulled on my beard.

"Now that's naughty son. Don't touch Santa's beard. I'll try to find you a puppy if you'll help your mom."

"Deal Santa." We shook hands.

The next girl wore a red dress decorated with white snow flakes. "I want a picture with you Santa." She smiled with several missing teeth. The store photographer Bert started taking

139

A Story A Day Keeps the EVIL Away

pictures. I felt something warm and wet. The girl peed on me!

When she joined her mom discussing all the expensive picture packages, I called my elves over. "Santa needs a break soon. I just got urinated on." One twin laughed; the other bit her lip to keep from laughing. Like I said before, the Santa suit came with two pairs of pants.

I took my cafeteria break in the late afternoon and found the turkey special. After lunch, the rest of the day moved quickly. Before long I changed clothes, wrote a note pinned onto the soiled Santa pants, and hurried through the blowing snow to my bus. I caught "Frosty the Snowman" on TV as I sipped my generic cola. I went to bed early.

Another day and another long line of kids wanting to see me. A lot of stores stopped having a store Santa Claus so Watkins got families traveling over an hour for Santa. If they spent some money in the department store, and they always did, all the better for business. The day passed surprisingly slow even though we had lots of kids. I found myself checking my watch a few times which I almost never did. Finally the last child stood in line, even my elves needed a break.

The boy came over and talked to me without sitting down. He stood about three feet tall, unkempt dark hair and sparkling hazel eyes. His long burgundy coat reached his knees. "What do you want for Christmas Santa?" His question surprised me.

"I guess I never thought about it. What's your name son?"

"Sebastian. Come on Santa. Answer my question."

"If you wanna know the truth Sebastian, I'm pretty lonely these days, no Mrs. Claus waiting for me at home."

My head spun around to see her walk into the room. She wore a black leather dress with matching black boots. Her grey fur coat was unbuttoned. When she smiled in my direction, I

A Gift for Santa

nearly fell on the floor. Her black hair flowed past her shoulders and those bright green eyes stared at me.

I turned to Sebastian. "That's an example of a woman who is out of my league, no chance."

Sebastian patted me on the back. "Never say never Santa."

She approached me! "Let me take you to dinner Santa."

Somehow I managed to say, "Just give me a minute to change clothes."

"No." She replied firmly. "I want to go out with Santa."

I followed her almost in a trance. "I don't get paid till Friday. So maybe we could have coffee."

She took my gloved hand. "I'm paying for dinner. I've always wanted to have dinner with Santa Claus."

We crossed the street to Devon's Diner. Before I opened my menu, she ordered, "Two steak dinners with everything. Two coffees and two pieces of peppermint pie."

Children sitting at other tables yelled excitedly, "Santa, Santa!" Fortunately their parents smiled and told them to "Let Santa eat his dinner." I waved to the happy children.

Then I tried to make conversation and not stare at her like a lovesick school boy. "You are beautiful. Sorry, I had to say it. You probably hear that all the time."

"Never from Santa. When I was a child, the stores would have breakfast with Santa. My parents could never afford for me to go. Now that I own a software company I can do anything I want."

The steak dinners arrived and I fought a losing battle trying to keep my white Santa beard clean. She laughed so I took that as a good sign. I could barely finish my pie. I stared into her hypnotic green eyes. "Can't remember when I've eaten such a great meal. Thanks."

A Story A Day Keeps the EVIL Away

She grabbed my hand. "Oh I'm not done with you Santa. You're coming with me."

We walked through the downtown streets as the snow fell lightly. When we reached the town square, red and green lights flashed on the Christmas trees around the gazebo. Standing inside the gazebo, a group of carolers entertained a small gathering of holiday shoppers. Children surrounded us and we sang along to the great Christmas songs. A magical moment I'll remember forever!

The next morning I woke up in my apartment still dressed in my Santa suit. I realized that I never asked her name. Did last night happen or was it a dream?

Back at Watkins Department Store, I watched the children come and go. Before I realized it, I started my second week as Santa Claus. That attractive woman never returned and I believed it never happened at all. Every year at the Christmas season I had a sense of loneliness. But I didn't discuss my feelings with anyone.

The Christmas countdown had begun. More people filled our store. Long lines of kids kept us working extra time especially on the weekends. At least we got paid overtime. Bev and Becky noticed my depression. "What's wrong Santa? You don't seem like your jolly old self."

"It's nothing girls. Thanks for asking. I do enjoy working with you every season." I noticed Sebastian standing alone in the line. "I got this girls. You can go home. I'll see you tomorrow."

Sebastian marched over to me. "Hey Santa, long day?"

"Yes. I haven't seen you in a while."

"I've been very busy with Christmas approaching." Sebastian seemed older than I remembered.

"You're not a child are you?" I guessed noticing his pointed

A Gift for Santa

ears for the first time.

"No. I work at the North Pole for the big guy in the red suit."

"You're kidding right?" I could hardly believe it.

"I travel around and try to make wishes come true at Christmas time. I thought I'd given you someone to take away the loneliness. You seem so sad Santa. How can I help?"

I felt a tear rolling down my cheek. "This one might be too big for you and the real Santa." I hesitated. Did I even want to discuss this with a stranger or an elf?

"Do you believe in Christmas miracles Bobby Richards?"

"When I was a little boy growing up in Ohio, I would wait up for Santa Claus and fall asleep on the couch. I guess Santa became my Christmas miracle every year till my older sister ruined everything telling me Santa didn't exist."

"You don't have to tell me anymore. I know about your son Ted."

I stood up and faced Sebastian. "I never mentioned Ted to anybody. Every year I buy him a Christmas present and put it on the shelf in my closet. It's been four years since I've seen him. His mother took him one day and disappeared. No letters, no phone calls. The police didn't help."

Sebastian gripped both of my gloved hands and called, "Ted, come and meet your father."

I saw my son too stunned to speak. A little taller than I remembered, same messy brown hair and soft blue eyes. Ted appeared happy and confused at the same time. I hugged my boy for the first time in four years and never wanted to let go. I removed my beard and Santa hat tossing them onto the throne seat. "There's so much I want to say to you, ask you Ted. I'm so happy you're here with me."

A Story A Day Keeps the EVIL Away

Then she entered my life again. "My two favorite men!" This time she dazzled in a floor length red dress covered up by a black leather coat. "I have a job offer to discuss with you Santa. It starts the day after Christmas. Let's get some dessert and discuss our future family." She wore my Santa hat. "My name's Holly."

Sebastian said as we strolled out of sight, "Merry Christmas to all and to all a good night."

Rose Among Thorns

In the misty morning Spencer jogged through Amity Park until he reached the fountain. Tulips of red, yellow, and white surrounded the fountain and announced the early spring season. None of this mattered to Spencer. He focused on the green bench where there was business to transact. But someone else sat on the bench, a young woman feeding the pigeons.

Sitting at the opposite end of the bench, Spencer glanced at the woman. He could judge people pretty quickly. A frayed white blouse, worn jeans and disheveled auburn hair painted the picture of a woman down on her luck. Divorced? Unemployed? Sad blue eyes returned his stare.

To engage in small talk would only delay his trip to the airport. Still, she represented an easy mark, a quick encounter before he left for Berlin, Paris, or wherever the instructions would send him this time. A hired gun traveled anywhere if the money was right. He diverted his eyes to the fountain. Hopefully, the woman was running out of bread to feed the pigeons. The three word message would contain all the information he needed.

A Story A Day Keeps the EVIL Away

But it remained underneath her side of the bench.

A simple two rings on his cell from that same number sent him to the park. It could occur every month or whenever his services were needed. He watched the water cascade from the angel statute in the middle of the fountain. The beauty of the falling water and of the multicolored tulips was lost on his grim face.

Spencer thought it for the best to walk away from the bench before he reached out to her physically or verbally. The fountain water reflected his burgundy jogging suit. It seemed like a silly disguise for him. Running always brought back the incident in Beirut where a bullet shattered his right knee nearly killing him in an exchange of gunfire. His knee was still sore after the short run in the park.

Finally, Spencer saw her reach for her Gucci purse, probably one of those thirty dollar ripoffs of the original. Turning back to the fountain, he never saw the pistol emerge from her purse. But he did feel the single bullet enter the back of his head. His body died instantly although his mind wondered why am I falling in the fountain?

Clouds of red blood encircled his dead body in the water.

She reached under the bench retrieving the secret paper. After watching him and following him to the park for six months, she knew the importance of the brief message. She tossed her auburn wig in the trash and left the park.

Near the East River an abandoned warehouse with underground parking and enough high tech toys for any covert operation was slated to be razed eight years ago but the yearly DC checks kept it open for business. "My favorite flower, Rose." Felix Walker smiled at the hippy chick with blonde hair reaching her butt. Her blue eyes turned to hazel.

"Don't my disguises ever surprise you?" She asked trying

Rose Among Thorns

to hide the disappointment in her voice.

"Not after five years together. How do you get past the facial recognition scan? That's a mystery!" Felix's computer nerd appearance easily hid the deadly skills he possessed. His shaved head, gold wire glasses and his normal wardrobe of t-shirts and jeans made him look like a Facebook intern.

Warren with his wild curly black hair joined them in the small office. In spite of his GQ daily clothing, the African American captain would rather fight than talk to anyone. Recovering from surgery for a sword wound, of all crazy injuries, kept him office bound. "Do you have it?"

"Of course." Rose produced the small paper and read aloud, "347, Duke, Light."

Warren guessed, "347 is the flight number?"

"Okay," Felix added. "Duke could be a reference to John Wayne or just Wayne. A contact or a target?"

"Better hope Wayne isn't Bruce Wayne. Batman would kick your ass Felix." Warren laughed.

Rose said, "Light, City of Light. We're going to Paris."

"Got it!" Felix looked up from his laptop. "Wellington Wayne, the black market arms dealer. He apparently pissed off somebody. That's Spencer's target."

Warren was the senior ranking officer but hated to give orders to them. "Felix, your ticket will be at the airport under Spencer's name. Rose, if we can't get you on the same plane, I'll find another flight. I'll text you."

They arrived at JFK International Airport separately. Felix used his fake Spencer ID to retrieve his ticket and a folded message saying, "Hyatt Paris." Felix found his seat and positioned the ear buds for the long flight ahead. He had to look up at the long legs and short black leather skirt walking down the aisle.

A Story A Day Keeps the EVIL Away

Rose! She did trick him this time. Only a smile passed between them.

Rose tried to sleep. When that didn't work, she checked out the recent movie choices available. Nothing held her attention although she selected two movies to watch. It had been over a year since she'd been in the field on assignment for the Agency. Mistakes now cost lives.

Shariff was only twenty-seven but he had a growing reputation as a worldwide terrorist. Like many orphans in the Middle East he learned explosives training at an early age losing a right pinkie finger and nearly his life to a homemade bomb. He became a fixture in terrorist training camps progressing from student to teacher before he reached the age of twenty. Then his reputation grew as an assassin. A knife, pistol, high-powered rifle whatever weapon would be most effective in the given situation and target. Shariff avoided traveling to Yemen. When the message came from Yoesf, he couldn't refuse his old friend. The training camps in Afghanistan drew them together. One day they fought each other in the sand to the delight of others; the next day they became brothers, a bond that stretched nine years. Shariff flipped through his many passports and decided to travel as a Turkish banker even wearing a linen suit for the plane ride.

In the shadow world of his business faces were important. A fake mustache, sunglasses, a hat didn't change the faces he studied. Someone caught his attention. An American with blend-in features, average height, weight, a bland expressionless face but one he had seen before. A passing car, a man walking past his apartment, that restaurant multiple times. How could he have been such a fool? He was being tracked by another professional.

Rose Among Thorns

When the flight landed at Aden International Airport, he grabbed his carry-on bag and found the airport restroom. Like a spider to a fly come follow me, he thought. Entering the first stall, he waited to see if he was really being singled out or was he just a little paranoid today.

The American entered walking to a urinal. Shariff observed the man heading over to the sink and began washing his hands. Shariff slowly approached him. It was all over in seconds. The American looked down at his hands. Then he glanced up, startled; a thin red line appeared on his throat. Blood started gushing from the knife wound. The American's head hit the sink as he fell to the restroom floor.

Shariff wiped his bloody knife on the man's jacket and returned it to his pocket. Next, he joined the other arriving passengers rushing to the waiting taxicabs. The large black American car roared in front of him. "Ahalan Shariff." A voice called out when the rear door flew open.

"Yoesf, why are we meeting here?"

"Driver, proceed slowly around the airport." He pushed up the soundproof divider. "A change of plans I'm afraid. Your services are needed in Paris."

"Paris?"

Yoesf was a large man who had gained weight as well as wealth over the years. Money opened a lot of doors and loosened tongues of secrets. He turned the small key revealing the contents of his attache case. Lifting the picture he showed it to Shariff. "Your assignment—Wellington Wayne." The picture showed a balding, dark complexioned face with a pencil-thin mustache and eyes like a large rat. "He has double-crossed our people in arms shipments."

"Why me? This is beneath my talents."

A Story A Day Keeps the EVIL Away

"We know Wayne is in Paris. Remember Spencer? A Western, a hired gun we use from time to time. Found murdered in New York hours ago. If Wayne is found talking with others, kill them all and get back to the airport quickly my friend." Yoesf looked deep into Shariff's dark eyes. "I trust you with my life Shariff. Here is your plane ticket. Wayne is registered under his own name at the Hyatt Regency. A bold man, a foolish man."

Yoesf wrapped on the divider and the car stopped. "Salaam Alekum my friend." Shariff spoke picking his bag off the car floor as he returned to the airport terminal.

At Charles de Gaulle Airport, Rose met Felix at the cab station. When the forty minute ride ended, they climbed out of the cab. Rose froze staring into the distance. "The Eiffel Tower is beautiful at night with all the lights."

Felix carried their suitcases. "That's right it's your first trip to Paris. You can ride to the top of the Eiffel Tower. If there's time tomorrow, we'll visit the Arc de Triomphe and walk down the Champs Elysées."

They checked in at the Hyatt front desk. Felix wrote a brief message handing it to the female clerk. "I need this delivered to Mr. Wellington Wayne tonight. Thank you." They rode the elevator to the twentieth floor. As they entered their room, Felix said, "I need some sleep. I can never relax on these night flights over the ocean."

"I'm taking a shower." Rose disappeared into the bathroom. Moments later the bathroom door opened.

"I texted Warren." Felix looked up from his cell. Rose emerged completely naked. Water glistened on her vibrant young body. "Damn you Rose!"

"You can sleep tomorrow." Rose laughed joining Felix in bed.

Rose Among Thorns

Rose stared at the full length mirror. Today's clothing required blending in with her surroundings. No outrageous colors or fashions. Faded jeans for comfort and a long black top to cover the gun in her waistband seemed right. The solid black baseball cap pulled down tight would keep her hair out of the way and hide her face too.

"What happened to the girl with the short skirt on last night's flight?" Felix wondered.

"Oh, she's back in the suitcase. This is my business attire." She gave him a sly smile. "Contacts not glasses today I see."

Felix wore his expensive navy suit with a white open collar shirt. "I'm meeting Wayne in Restaurant la Fayette off the lobby. He doesn't know me so I thought a public place would be the best. Remember, stay out of sight. We need to guide Wayne to a safe house before someone else comes gunning for him."

They carried their suitcases to the lobby and left them, with a generous tip, at the bellman's station. Felix entered the restaurant sitting by the large windows with a view of the Eiffel Tower. Rose sat at a corner table with the perfect sight lines to observe the meeting.

Felix stirred the spoon of sugar into his coffee. A heavyset man in a grey suit approached the table looking from side to side. Nervously he asked, "Are you Felix Walker?"

"Yes. Please have a seat. Coffee Mr. Wayne?" Felix signaled for the waiter.

"I prefer hot tea." He hesitated until the waiter returned to the kitchen. "What is the meaning of this? I don't know you Mr. Walker."

"I'm like your guardian angel. We intercepted a message. There's been a contract taken out on your life. We want to keep you alive."

A Story A Day Keeps the EVIL Away

"As do I." The waiter placed the cup of tea in front of Wayne and left. "I've been advised to stay out of Middle East politics. But there's lots of money paid to arms dealers like myself."

Felix sipped his coffee. "I don't agree with your politics sir. We need..." He never finished his sentence.

A man dressed as a waiter ran towards them with an AK-47 blasting away. Felix's hand dropped his gun as he fell to the floor. Wayne collapsed onto the table. Cups and saucers broke apart from the gunfire.

Rose reacted faster than her dead partner. Jumping over a table, she nearly slipped in the growing pools of blood on the carpeted floor. She ran to the kitchen knocking chairs out of her way. Her pistol was gripped tightly in her right hand. Fortunately, only a skeleton crew worked the morning shift. She easily ran past them through the metal pans balanced on the large cooking surfaces and the open metal drawers filled with colorful produce. Her target changed before her eyes. She stepped on the waiter's red jacket and saw the AK-47 tossed aside.

Suddenly, Rose found herself in an alley outside of the hotel. She managed to fire one shot at the fleeing man in the white shirt. But it hit his left shoulder briefly spinning him around long enough for Rose to see his face. Could it be Shariff? The legendary assassin had traveled to Paris.

Rose closed the distance between them. Shariff rushed through the early morning traffic and into the underground parking garage across the street. Ignoring the loud honking from a cab driver, Rose followed him. A bullet zipped past Rose's right ear from a concrete barrier. Then the sound of running returned.

She had to stay close. Felix would not be backing her and

Rose Among Thorns

Warren remained in New York. Would her training and limited field experience be enough to catch a professional hit man? She fired wildly at Shariff hearing the bullets ricochet off the hood of a white Porsche. He disappeared. Rose walked slowly going car to car checking around and under a long line of cars. Where was he? At least he wore a white shirt. Eventually, there would be a trail of his blood to follow.

Three more cars were left in the row. A right hand jumped towards her from under the car wielding a deadly blade. She kicked repeatedly at his hand while avoiding being stabbed. Suddenly her leg was cut as her shoe finally knocked the knife harmlessly into the air. Shariff raced down to the next lower level of the garage. No time to worry about the blood appearing on her jeans by her right calf. She fought through the pain firing two more shots.

A voice cried out in pain. Could it be a trap? Rose stood over Shariff's body face down on the concrete. Two bullet holes were visible on his back. Was he dead? As she caught a slight movement from his right arm, she emptied her gun into his body. Mistakes cost lives. Not hers but Felix's. She collapsed on the concrete floor and looked at her cut leg. Tearing off part of her shirt, she tied the wound. She began to limp out of the garage, out of the Hyatt, out of Paris.

A Story A Day Keeps the EVIL Away

PROTO

Was a time when people flocked from miles round to witness Tevin. His stories, his revelations 'bout our world became popular when Tevin grew out of his teens into a fine young man. And being near seven feet he commanded attention right there. Sure, that included sympathy for his missing left hand. Tevin held court anywhere from Bess Diner to that rundown gas station where the G and S lit up at night.

People crossed through the Broken Blue Mountains to hear Tevin speak. Good old Broken Blue had a gap in the middle near half-mile wide where people could come and go as they pleased. They would listen to every story he told and they brought their families and friends too.

I recall one special night when hundreds of people gathered covering the hillside like dandelions in the spring. That smooth, honey-sounding voice spoke, "Remember that comet we all saw last night?" Tevin paused. They were in the palm of his hand and he didn't notice or care. His boyish charm drew them in. "Bright light that jumped cross the sky. Some of you ran outside to watch. And some of you probably hid under your

A Story A Day Keeps the EVIL Away

beds." He chuckled lightly. The crowd laughed with him. "All those twinkling stars you see in the night sky, folks live there. Like me and you, even Old Patch."

That's when I nodded to Tevin for the acknowledgement, stood and bowed to the amused crowd. "Millions and millions of people living their lives, gotta be at least one Old Patch! Let's wave to the stars. One, two, three, WAVE." Hundreds of arms reached high into the air waving.

The excitement ended kinda sudden when someone yelled, "Tell us 'bout those folks Tevin. Are they just like us? Please tell us."

Don't know exactly what got into the boy's mind right then. Must have been something real dark. I sat close enough to the top of the hill to see that tear rolling down his cheek. Looked like other tears were 'bout to follow. His smile faded. Tevin faced the large gathering and said, "I can't talk about those people. Can't do it. I gotta go." Suddenly, he walked away from us heading down the other side of the hill.

We all waited. Was it a joke or an act of some sort? Hushed voices responded, "Where is he?" "Is he coming back?" "Should we wait for him?" "Nothing wrong with that question to upset him so." Slowly the stunned people rose in small groups heading back to their homes.

Guess I became one of the last dozen or so to leave. Tevin's behavior puzzled us. Never saw him sad or troubled before. I decided to leave him to his thoughts. Maybe try and visit him tomorrow.

But tomorrow stretched into a week. No one had seen him. I sat in Bess Diner. Oma, my favorite waitress, approached the table. She was missing two fingers on her left hand. Didn't stop her from juggling the plates and cups from the counter to

PROTO

the waiting tables. "You must know something 'bout Tevin, Old Patch." I got used to that nickname 'cause of that patch covering my right eye since birth and I earned the old part by living too long.

"Haven't seen him. Sorry Oma. How's Royar working out in the kitchen?"

"Our one-legged chief. Really he's amazing. He can cook anything on that stool by the stove. Just needs help getting on and off his crutches. Bess is always round handing him ingredients or reading orders to him. Don't know where we'd be without him."

Aber rushed into the diner right to my table. "Did you hear? Did you hear?" Aber liked to repeat everything like you didn't hear him the first time. He even had two colors of hair, brown in the front and yellow in the back of his head. "Tevin's coming tomorrow night. Tevin's coming tomorrow night."

"Is there an echo in here?" Nobody responded to my attempt at humor. But the lunch crowd immediately began buzzing about Tevin's return to his adoring public.

Apparently, Tevin wanted a small group, not all the outsiders from across the mountains. Our townspeople spread the news. When the blessed event arrived, I wished I had sold tickets. Folks filled the restaurant and the remaining people stood or sat outside to hear his talk. I swear the whole town showed up that night.

Tevin appeared from the kitchen to wild applause. Our town could forgive or forget his last event. I've known the boy 'bout his whole life. Knew his parents too. That's why I could tell he forced a smile, betrayed by his sad, one blue one brown, eyes.

"Let's start with your questions for me," Tevin began.

157

A Story A Day Keeps the EVIL Away

Oma wore her blue work apron. She said loudly, "Why does the weather change near every day?"

"We're just lucky, I guess," Tevin replied with a real smile this time. "Snow today, 75 yesterday. Who knows what we'll get tomorrow?"

A voice from the back by the door, "Answer her question. Or don't you know the answer."

"Oh, I do know why. Let's not ruin this snowy evening." He seemed to be fighting back tears again.

Aber asked, "Why is life so hard? Why is life so hard?"

"Not sure what you mean Aber." Tevin looked confused.

A large man pushed away his chair and announced, "I know what Aber's getting at. Crops barely grow. We got townspeople missing arms, legs, fingers or hands like you Tevin. Life is hard. Explain that to us Tevin!"

A young woman added, "We got beaches that are half sand and half rocks. And the small fish provide us with little to eat."

An elderly man shouted angrily, "How 'bout day and night? Some days stay real light into the late evening. Both suns are out at the same time. Then the next day is nearly dark all day. How come?"

Tevin covered his eyes with his right hand hoping that whatever troubled him would vanish. "Questions were a mistake. I'm sorry." He lowered his hand and continued in a serious tone, "You don't want the truth. Trust me. You don't want to know." He turned towards the kitchen and another early exit.

"Don't leave us yet," Oma begged. "Tell us the truth!"

"Please Tevin." The disappointed crowd reacted. But he disappeared. I finished my coffee and walked through the crowded room.

"Show's over folks," I announced. The questions that night did trouble me some. Took me awhile to fall asleep. I did wonder why the world we lived in was such a mess. Kinda got used to our broken lives thinking, it is what it is.

To my surprise and I'm sure everyone else's too, signs appeared all over town. "THE TRUTH TONIGHT—Tevin returns for the final time at Bess Diner."

Again, with the unpredictable weather, we had a sunny day. The snow melted. It turned into a nice summer night. The daylight extended into the night, a bonus for our special evening. Guess our twin suns wanted to hear Tevin too. Bess Diner moved chairs and tables outside. Bess got Zelo to bring over chairs from Hunter's Lodge down the street. People even brought blankets and their own lawn chairs.

The anticipation enveloped our little town. To hear Tevin again and the real truth 'bout our world represented the best and worse news possible. Some parents left their kids at home. What would he tell us? I remained silent but chatter surrounded me 'bout Tevin's revelations for us, "I'm excited and frightened." "I want the truth." "Scared, guess I'm scared." "If Tevin knows, we all need to know the truth."

Tevin arrived dressed in black from his black hooded sweatshirt to his black pants and boots. This Tevin had never spoken to us before. He reached his arms in the air and no one made a sound.

"I have something that needs to be said," Tevin began. "It's not fair for you to live your lives with no answers to all your questions about life. This is the ultimate secret. When my parents passed down the secret to me, generations of my family knew the truth. No one else has heard the real truth."

Tevin wiped away his tears with the back of his right hand.

A Story A Day Keeps the EVIL Away

"The name of our planet is Proto, meaning the first. I'm sure some of you thought about the name from time to time. When the supreme being created life, it began here. Of all the billions of planets and universes, life started here."

The people waited with anticipation for each word. Tevin continued, "This was the practice planet. Like the Broken Blue Mountains that seem incomplete, practice. The hot, cold weather—more practice. Why are some of us missing body parts like our ancestors before us? Practice. The supreme being had to learn how to create. But that's not my news."

He paused and looked up to the star-filled sky. "No, the real secret is the supreme being left us. The giant shadow that the ancients refer to as the Darkest Night was the supreme being turning his back to us and walking away. More worlds, more universes, new life needed to be created. The supreme being abandoned us. We are completely on our own."

Back from the Dead?

The taste of blood filled her mouth, a familiar taste. Did Blake break her nose again? No severe pain on her face appeared this time. Blake rushed towards her. She woke up screaming. Searching through her tears, she knew he couldn't be there. Blake died in a fiery crash. Still, she felt his presence everywhere she turned in the house.

A relaxing shower seemed to help. Megan closed her brown eyes as she shampooed her short, jet black hair. HE WAS THERE! Whenever her eyes blinked, his crew cut, his angry face with the piercing grey eyes would not leave her. The large frame of muscles that had once attracted her instead represented terror, fear and pain.

She caught her body shaking over morning coffee. Six long years of physical abuse and mental anguish had left her frightened and scared. Her new life started now. Had the nightmare really ended? Time to rid the house of Blake's belongings. She loved living here but would all the bad memories force her to sell the house?

There was a knock at the side door. Her first reaction

A Story A Day Keeps the EVIL Away

caused her to shake uncontrollably. Then she noticed her neighbor, Gwen. She opened the door saying, "Gwen, I'm happy to see you."

Gwen's curly blond hair and expressive blue eyes matched her alluring shape. She marched in clutching a box of trash bags. "Is today the day? I'm ready to help you get that bastard's crap out of your house."

"Thanks. Please sit and have some coffee." She poured her a cup joining her at the small kitchen table.

"Megan, are you having those dreams? You look tired." She added a spoon of sugar to the coffee.

"Blake might have left the world but not my dreams. I'm trying to avoid taking the sleeping pills again."

"You need a good night's sleep."

Megan jumped when the door bell rang. She found a Western Union man at the front door.

"Telegraph miss. Sign here." He retrieved the pen from her. Handing her the telegraph he added, "Thanks. Have a good day."

Gwen heard the door close followed by a loud crash. She ran around the corner to find Megan passed out on the floor. Lifting the telegraph from the carpet, she read, "I'll be seeing you. Blake."

She managed to help Megan to the couch. "Megan. Megan honey are you alright?"

Megan's brown eyes slowly blinked open. Where was Blake? Gwen's friendly face greeted her instead. "Is Blake here? Where is he?" Her whole body shook as Gwen gave her a reassuring hug.

"Somebody's playing a cruel joke on you. Everything's okay. I'll get your coffee."

Back from the Dead?

"Please just sit with me Gwen." They sat quietly for several minutes. "Maybe he's not dead. There's no proof he was even in that car."

"Blake's dead. He left the bar driving his Corvette. Witnesses from the bar gave written statements to the police."

"But the car exploded. Even his dental records couldn't be used. What if he didn't die and someone else carjacked the Corvette?"

"Stop it!" Gwen said firmly. "You'll drive yourself crazy. He's dead, end of story. Let's go back to the kitchen and finish our coffee."

They sat with their coffee mugs with Gwen talking and refilling their coffee. "I know the next thing you're gonna say. Your anniversary is in two days. Forget this nonsense. Let's go shopping and out to lunch. Spend some of that money from his life insurance policy. Maybe that will cheer you up."

Reluctantly, Megan grabbed her purse and set her home security system. "This might be what I need the most." She looked in the mirror and brushed her short black hair. Her sad brown eyes stared back at her. "Let's go."

Hours of shopping and eating passed as Gwen pulled her Chevy into Megan's driveway. "I'll help you carry your bags," she volunteered. Gwen scooped up the two overflowing Macy's bags. Megan punched in her alarm code after she entered the house. She tossed the bag of shoe boxes on the table.

Gwen came in laughing, "White wine with salad, what a great combination! And the brownies didn't hurt either." Suddenly they both stopped and stared at the black roses covering the kitchen counter. A small card stated, "Happy Anniversary. I'll be seeing you soon. Blake."

Megan couldn't stop shaking. She gripped Gwen's hands

A Story A Day Keeps the EVIL Away

tightly in hers. "Now do you believe me. Blake's alive! Who else would know the security code and walk right in? I'm scared Gwen."

"Let's go to the police." Gwen led her to the door.

Detective Malloy greeted the two women ushering them to the wooden chairs by his desk. "How can I help you ladies?" Life didn't seem fair, he thought. I finally get the attention of two attractive women when my gut is expanding and my hair is disappearing. Where were they twenty years ago?

"This will sound crazy detective," Megan began.

"Trust me I've heard them all." He smiled.

"My dead husband isn't dead! He's terrorizing me!" Tears welled in her brown eyes.

Gwen interrupted, "Someone is threatening her. Maybe or maybe not her husband. She received a telegraph this morning and dead roses this afternoon from her late husband Blake."

Detective Malloy started jotting down notes. "Let me get some basic information. His name is Blake. How and when did he die?"

Gwen looked at her friend's tears. She answered for her, "Blake Clemons. He died in a car accident ten days ago over on Franklin Avenue."

"He's not dead!" Megan screamed through her tears. "He walked in my house with my security system on! How else could that happen?"

"Calm down." Malloy handed her a Kleenex. "I would suggest buying a hidden camera. You can find them anywhere. Set it up and spend the night at your friend's house."

Between them they mounted the camera and checked it twice. This time Megan took a sleeping pill in Gwen's spare bedroom producing her first night of sleep in a week. But a

Back from the Dead?

disturbing image of a fist, Blake's fist, smashing into her jaw woke her like an ice cold shower.

Gwen opened the bedroom door to Megan's screams. "Are you alright Megan?"

"Yes. Yes, I'm fine. Sorry for waking you. I wanna check that camera. I have to know if it recorded Blake."

Within an hour they hurried across the street to Megan's house. Megan punched in the alarm code. Gwen stood on a chair and retrieved the small camera. Playing through the tape—He appeared! "Gwen, it's him!" Megan yelled. The black leather jacket, dark jeans, cowboy boots represented his usual style.

Gwen put her arm around Megan's shoulders. "You can't tell. It's from the back you can't see his face."

"It's him. I was married to him for six years. Who else could it be?" Megan sat down and fought to regain her breath.

Gwen pulled out Malloy's card and called. "Detective, can you come over to Megan's house? We need your help. Thanks." They waited with Megan gripping Gwen's hands tightly. The sound of a car door slamming, Gwen rose to open the side door. A second sound enveloped the first with cries for help.

As Gwen opened the door, Detective Malloy's bloody body fell forward nearly knocking her over. He gasped trying to form words in his final moments. Stab wounds on his back filled with blood. Gwen screamed.

Megan reached the side door, stared at Malloy's dead body and collapsed on the kitchen floor. Gwen ran for her cell calling 911. "Send the police! We have a dead police detective and a killer loose in our neighborhood!"

Police patrol cars zoomed down the street closing it to all traffic. Two officers entered the house followed by the

A Story A Day Keeps the EVIL Away

paramedics. Gwen answered questions while Megan ran through a quick check by the paramedics. The next wave of people included Briggs, a salty, unhappy veteran detective and four forensics men. Megan and Gwen responded to the same questions for the third time. Megan searched and found a picture of Blake for Detective Briggs. "This case is personal," Briggs explained. "I've worked with Detective Malloy for seventeen years. Our families have vacationed together. I'll find this man whether it's Blake Clemons or someone else."

"Thanks detective." Megan walked him to the front door.

"Here's my card Megan. You call me day or night understand?"

Gwen sat with Megan on the living room couch as the forensic team finished and left the house. "Can I ask you a question?" Gwen continued,"What do you know about Blake's family?"

"Nothing. He wouldn't discuss it. I know he lived in Naples, Florida for awhile."

"Anything out of the ordinary happen after Blake's funeral?"

"I discovered a key for a safety deposit box at Cardinal Savings. I found an empty box like someone got there before me." Megan responded.

"Did you question the bank employees?"

Megan shook her head. "They saw Blake apparently off and on. Me they've never seen. I didn't even know about the safety deposit box."

Gwen said, "I'll call Briggs about Blake living in Florida. Maybe there's family to contact." She grabbed her purse. "I'm going home. Call me if you need me."

Megan tried to be brave as she watched Gwen cross the

Back from the Dead?

street. There would be no sleep in her future. How could she ever relax and close her eyes? Blake seemed to be everywhere she looked. And Malloy's blood remained by the side door. Twilight turned to night. Megan had all the lights on throughout the house. Briggs had promised her a patrol car driving by every hour. She watched it pass her house again.

She refilled her wine glass and turned on the TV. Any diversion would help. Television ranged from stupid reality shows to bloody crime dramas. She switched to the local news. There Was Her House! The murdered police detective. The patrol cars covering the street. She couldn't take anymore. The night became her only companion. Fear gripped her in the darkness. Blake lived in the night waiting to terrorize her whenever he wanted to. A combination of the third glass of wine and sheer exhaustion, Megan passed out on the couch.

Megan woke to a ringing cell phone. Briggs. "Yes detective. Is there anything new?"

"Gwen called me about Blake's connection to Naples, Florida. Turns out there are living family members. Gotta a friend in Florida who owes me a favor. I'll let you know what he finds."

"We'll talk later today." Megan showered and dressed. She had made one decision—to sell the house. If she had any doubts, Malloy's murder forced her decision. Megan realized that she hadn't eaten in nearly twenty-four hours. She reached for the eggs but associated eggs with Blake. Why couldn't he leave her alone? A cinnamon bagel and orange juice tasted like a feast to her.

Gwen wisely came to the front door. Neither of them wanted to dwell on the image of Malloy's dead body by the side door. "I stopped at Starbucks. Got your favorite," she said

A Story A Day Keeps the EVIL Away

handing her the cup. "I also brought this." She revealed a small gun in her purse.

"You have a gun?"

"When Wayne moved out, he left it for my protection. One of the few kind things that bastard ever did for me."

They sat in the kitchen. Megan caught herself laughing at Gwen's comments. When was the last time she laughed out loud? For the first time in days she began to relax. "I'm selling the house," Megan spoke.

"You can't leave me. Don't decide today. Give it some time."

Megan's cell rang. "Briggs?"

"Stay in your house. I'm in my car heading there now. Don't answer the door to anyone!"

Megan raced to the living room with Gwen close behind. "Oh My God, it's Blake!" The large man walked briskly up the sidewalk to the front door. Gwen screamed and reached for her gun. But Megan stood and watched. Same height, crew cut, muscular build. Where was the tattoo of the tiger on his left forearm? Not Blake?

His boot crashed repeatedly into the wooden door. The frame shattered apart. The door flew open. The man ran directly at Megan. Gwen fired and fired until the man fell to his knees before dropping dead at their feet.

Detective Briggs took the gun from Gwen's shaking hand. Police sirens filled the air. Police officers hurried into the living room. The paramedics joined the police with a stretcher.

Briggs ushered the women to the kitchen. "I just received a return call from my contact in Florida. Blake was an identical twin. As far as I can tell, they both moved up here. Had some blood oath between them. If anything happened to one, the

Back from the Dead?

other would seek revenge."

Megan sobbed, "But I didn't kill Blake!"

"His brother Bryan never knew or cared how Blake died. Bryan followed Blake's orders left behind in a safety deposit box full of cash."

"Detective Briggs," Megan asked in a frightened voice, "tell me they're not triplets!"

A Story A Day Keeps the EVIL Away

The Other Side

I heard it again louder this time. A scraping, clawing sound on the cabin door had interrupted my sleep. I kept silent not wanting to upset Gabriella asleep next to me. So I laid there staring at the wooden door. What was waiting in the night? I feared the answer to my own question. I needed to be strong for Gabriella even though I felt weak and scared.

When Gabriella, or Gabby as she preferred, slowly woke, kissed me, and headed to the bathroom, I sat up in bed. I felt beads of sweat covering my forehead. The noise returned! A pounding sound accompanied the clawing this time. Something large wanted to force itself into the cabin! How strong was a wooden cabin door?

I nearly jumped from the bed when Gabby swung open the bathroom door. A towel never looked so good. Her wet black hair reached her shoulders. Gabby's tall, fit figure pulled my attention away from the door. "Should I drop my towel?" She teased. "Maybe that'll put a smile back on your face Lucas."

"Sorry." I tried to reel in my fear. "I heard something outside the door. It freaked me out."

A Story A Day Keeps the EVIL Away

"Well lover, all our belongings are in the truck including our food. We need to go outside."

"Not now. Wait awhile. Whatever it is will go away on its own." I reasoned.

She gave me one of her alluring smiles. Her warm brown eyes made it hard to refuse her anything. "Our bags would already be in the cabin if you hadn't been in such a hurry to get me in bed last night."

I laughed. "Didn't hear any complaints from you last night. Or early this morning either."

Her smile held my focus until a loud thud crashed into the door. Gabby screamed, "Lucas what is it?"

"I don't know for sure. A grizzly bear?"

"Well I'm getting dressed." She left the room returning to the bathroom.

I picked yesterday's clothes off the floor, the new plaid shirt and my favorite jeans. Being clothed made me feel slightly better than dealing with the unknown threat while I was naked.

The clawing increased on the cabin door.

Gabby entered combing out her wet hair. "If you're afraid to go out there, give me your keys. I need my suitcase." Her bright pink t-shirt and black jeans still looked clean.

"No. Forget about it. Don't you remember the story Rick told us?"

"His bear story. You believed him?"

I explained, "Rick's hiked in this Alaskan wilderness before. One of the rangers told him about a giant brown grizzly bear the rangers named Big Mama. She got separated from her two cubs and mauled a family of four who camped there."

"Then the bear's killing continued," Gabby added almost bored.

The Other Side

"An animal acquires a taste for human blood after it's devoured a person. Anyway, Rick said seven more people were torn apart before they tracked the bear deep in the wooded hillside and shot it to death."

Gabby marched to the door. "I'm going to the truck. Lucas, are you coming with me?" Suddenly, she jumped back from the door when the loud noise started again.

"Sit down." I walked over to the small kitchen. "Let's see if Rick left us anything to eat." I opened cupboard doors. "I could make instant coffee. But I don't see any food."

"Forget it." She sat on a kitchen chair. "Now Starbucks I can drink. Not that instant crap."

I poured a glass of water and downed it quickly. I noticed my right hand shook and didn't want Gabby to see.

Gabby said, "Back to Rick, I remember the first time I met Ricky. I'd heard about the Paradise Lounge, the most exclusive place to be. I stopped after work with my friend Nancy. Ricky held court at a large round table filled with laughter and pretty girls. Somehow he spotted me staring at him."

"You still have feelings for him don't you?"

She ignored my remarks and continued, "There Rick sat in a black silk suit, white shirt and that big head of black hair. He took my breath away, I admit it. He invited me to his table and sent the other girls home. I completely forgot about Nancy till the next day at work. Even though she wouldn't forgive me for ditching her that night, she had a lot of questions about Ricky."

"When did you find out the truth about the real Rick?" I asked.

"We dated for weeks. Ricky would brag about robberies and being hooked up with the mob. I believed every story and that scared me. I was afraid to break up with him. Then I

A Story A Day Keeps the EVIL Away

learned about his cruel sense of humor. He would do anything for a joke no matter how tasteless or dangerous."

Did I hear a loud scraping sound on the door again?

She appeared to either not hear it or not react to it. She spoke, "When I met you at the Paradise Lounge, I thought you were a violent criminal like Rick."

I shook my head. "No, don't confuse me with my friends. I'm only the getaway driver. Never carried a gun and don't own one. I'm the wheel man. I just drive the car."

She raised her hands into fists. "Maybe I can beat you up and throw your body to the grizzly bear outside." She laughed. "How big do those bears get?"

"Rick told me as tall as eight feet and seven to eight hundred pounds." I lifted the steak knife from the silverware drawer. "I don't think this will protect us from something that large."

Gabby added, "Rick introduced us at the Paradise Lounge. That became a special night for me, for us. You wore a grey suit, blue shirt and that winning smile." She stared as if reliving the moment. "We had instant chemistry. Talking and drinking the night away, I dragged you onto the dance floor."

"I told you I couldn't dance." I smiled at the memory. "That short red dress, your long legs, I'll never forget that night." I leaned towards her and kissed her on the lips.

Changing the subject, Gabby said, "I talked you into this hiking trip. Rick gave us his cabin for the weekend." Then she stood. "I'm hungry. Let's get the cooler out of the truck."

I looked sideways at the cabin door. "Not yet. It's not safe." My feet refused to move.

"Afraid of a little old bear?" She walked towards the door. "Man up Lucas. It's probably run off by now."

The Other Side

I ran to the door and placed myself between Gabby and the door. I heard the clawing sound behind me and started shaking. "Okay, I'm afraid of what's on the other side."

"Yogi Bear is waiting out there." She laughed at me. "I'll wait for a few more minutes but that's all."

We both sat down. I said, "You know I didn't wanna go on this trip. I'm a city guy. I'd rather see bright lights and pavement than moonlight and trees."

"I love the outdoors Lucas. I even helped you shop for hiking boots and the right clothes to wear." Our eyes met. "I want you to enjoy this weekend."

I was quiet picturing some large brown creature that would devour us. Why did I agree to this stupid trip? One look at Gabriella and all my doubts seemed to disappear. If only that monster would leave us alone.

She grabbed my keys off the kitchen counter. "I'll run to the truck and right back inside. It'll only take a minute."

Standing beside her, I said, "Would you reconsider? Wait awhile longer?" I feared for her life as well as my own.

"You can stand by the door and watch me." Gabby opened the cabin door. She ran to the right out of my line of sight. I took a deep breath. Maybe I did overreact.

"I'm okay," she yelled. "There's nothing..." Suddenly her words turned into loud screams. Then no sound at all.

I slammed the door shut collapsing on the floor. I couldn't stop shaking. Tears flowed freely from my eyes. "Gabby, Gabby, I'm so sorry!" I kept repeating. Gabby dead! Torn apart by that damn bear!

I had to leave the cabin.

Would the bear be "occupied" making a meal out of dear Gabby? It might be my only chance to get out of the cabin.

175

A Story A Day Keeps the EVIL Away

If a bear tastes human blood...I tried to ignore my limited knowledge of bears. I ran to the kitchen and found two steak knives for weapons. It would have to do.

My vision was blurred by tears. But whatever courage I had left would desert me forever if I didn't act. Now or never!

I held a steak knife in each hand. I opened the door.

My eyes caught sight of big brown fur. I raced forward with renewed energy. Stabbing and stabbing the brown fur until it turned red and fell on the ground. A voice yelled, "STOP LUCAS STOP!" Gabby? "It's Rick dressed up as a bear. Lucas, we tried to play a joke on you!"

My hands were covered in blood. When an animal acquires a taste for human blood...I turned towards Gabby.

The Moment

Awkward teens
sharing dreams
of tomorrows.
The first kiss together
the pledge of forever.
The Moment We Met.

Wedding bells chime
the best man rhymes
of new beginnings.
A baby's cry
the years pass by.
The Moment Two Became Three.

We moved away
a new home to stay
for our family.
Retirement plans now
we'll adjust somehow.
The Moment We Grew Old.

The doctor's advice
the surgery twice
of a serious nature.
We said our goodbyes
the hugs, the cries.
The Moment I Lost You.

ABOUT THE AUTHOR

"Woll, yea I like the guy. Where would I be without him?"
—*Detective Sullivan*

"Michael better write me into another story or I'll make him disappear."
—*The Great Waldini*

"Woll's the writer? I didn't know that. I wish I'd met him first."
—*Isabella*

"This man is guilty of excitement and adventure. He is hereby sentenced to write another book—soon!"
—*Judge Potter*

Made in the USA
Columbia, SC
10 December 2017